i

Other Books by CR Wilson

Novel

"Deep in the Hearts of Texans"

Short Stories

"Many Trails"

"Just in Time for Christmas"

"For Love or Money"

"It Was For Love" (The Sequel to "For Love or Money")

"Gabe Harrison, Frontiersman" * the series

(Gabe's Law)   (The Comancheros)   (Across the River)

"Hezekiah Daly, Comanche Killer"

Novellas

"Moon on the River"

"The Many Trails of Garrett Marshall"

"The Strange Husband"

"Joe Morgan   Saint or Sinner"

"The Journal of Snow Woman"

Available on Amazon and Kindle e-Books

The Days of Rains

(The Legend of Johnny Rains)

CR Wilson

Author / Self-Publisher

Edited by Grace Sutton

ISBN – 13 : 978 1500 104757
ISBN – 10 : 1500104752

Special thanks to my wife, Cindy,
for all her help and thoughts.

This story contains some facts of actual events and persons. These were added to give historical setting of life in the Old West. All other characters portrayed herein are fictional.

The Songs

Lonely Cowboy (with a Dream that Rides Along)"

And

"Everything Reminds Me of You"

Lyrics were written by author CR Wilson
Copyright 2012

Table of Content

Prologue

The year is 1868. The War Between the States has been over for three years. The peace that the nation had longed for has not come. In the South, the carpetbaggers are making their living off the miseries of the defeated and destitute Southerners. The Negroes are unable to handle the new freedom given them and are still not accepted on equal terms with the white Southerners. In the North, jobs are hard to find for many of the soldiers returning home after serving their country. Conflict and unrest are found throughout the states. The western expansion is in full swing, giving to many the open land and the opportunity to begin a new life. Many good, hard-working men have brought their families and all they have to start a new life in lands of the west. But, as always, with the good comes the riffraff that feeds off the toil and sweat of the good. Many of them, soldiers of both the blue and the gray, having lived years of fighting and killing, have accepted it as a way of life. Many because they found it easier. Some just seemed to like that way of life. Among these are the James boys, the Youngers, and their like, who prey on the hard work of others and leave a trail of death and suffering along the way. Some of the good people who are trying to make a decent life for themselves and their families get caught up in the midst of things that change their lives completely. This is the story of one man, Trace Williams, and how his life changes from a young, gentle farmer into a legend as one of the fastest and deadliest men of the West.

Chapter One

Meeting the Strangers

Southern Indiana, mid-April, the land is back to life and the sun is warm on the good farm lands with low rolling hills. A few lazy clouds float across the pale blue sky with a southwest breeze adding to the warmth. A wagon is slowly rolling towards town carrying two young people. The girl is Carrie Johnston, seventeen years old, with blond hair, blue eyes and her face aglow as she chatters on as a girl seventeen and in love will. The boy, Trace Williams, also seventeen, is tall and rawboned with thick dark hair and grayish blue eyes; his build shows his younger years of hard work on his parents' farm. He has a gentle smile as he listens to Carrie's chattering. His dreams are that someday soon this girl he loves so much will be his wife. She is the most popular girl in the county at the church socials; like the one they're going to today. All the young men would like the chance to share lunch with Carrie, but they all know there is no chance for Trace Williams has her heart. It is understood by all that soon these two young people will be joined together as man and wife. As children there was no doubt by either parents, that these two would marry. While their fathers were away fighting in the war, many times Trace worked from sun up to way past dark to keep the farms up. He gave the same attention to the Johnston farm as he did his own dad's farm. What their parents told them was, that they would be given sections of the farms for themselves. It would be in the middle where the two farms met. Eventually, they would take over the two farms anyway since they were the only child in each family. The Johnstons thought of Trace as a son for years now; the same as the Williams thought of Carrie as a daughter. Sara and Harry Johnston would be stopping by to bring Sally and Tom Williams to the church social with them, saving wear and tear on a wagon and team of horses while enjoying each other's company.

As they traveled down the road towards town, Trace and Carrie saw two strangers coming their way. The two stopped as Trace pulled the reins on the horses and pulled the wagon to a stop to speak to them.

"Hi, new to this area, aren't you?" Trace spoke, in his soft friendly manner, trying to show friendship to the two.

"Yeah, boy, we're just passing through. Is there a town anywhere up this road?" The one stranger inquired with a friendly smile on his face.

"If you turn and follow us, there's a turn to the south you passed about a mile back. A couple of miles down the road is Salem. That's where we're going. The church social's today, there'll be great food and a lot of fun. There're friendly people there; they'd make you feel welcome and feed you real good. Would be worth the ride back."

"No, we're headed west. The land of opportunity. We'll just keep riding. Maybe someone will take pity on some poor ex-soldiers and feed us some grub. Any homes up that way that's not too far?" The one man seemed to do all the talking; the other just kind of set back and watched Trace and Carrie.

"You're in luck. Our farm is just a few miles up the road; then a few more miles is Carrie's home. If you hurry you can catch my folks before they leave, and I'm sure Ma will fix you up something to eat and something to take with you till you hit another town. She baked a lot of pies for the social and I'd bet she'll be giving you one of them, too." Trace knew his mother and dad would not deny food to any strangers passing by. "I just shot a buck the other day, so she'll have meat to share with you."

"You're sure they're that willing to share?" The man said, still showing a friendly smile.

"His folks are the nicest you'll find anywhere; that's why he's the best you'll find anywhere." Carrie hung on to Trace's arm.

"You shot the buck, huh; you're the hunter of the family?" The stranger seemed to enjoy the friendly conversation. "You a good shot, boy?"

"When he was only twelve, Morgan's raiders were heading this way. He went with the men to stop them. All the men said that he fought as good and brave as any of the men." Carrie just beamed as she bragged on Trace and his bravery and ability.

"You fought against Morgan and his men? They were a pretty tough bunch. Took a lot of nerve for a boy to go up against them."

"I was always big for my age; the men thought I was fourteen or fifteen. I wish I didn't have to do it. It wasn't the best feeling to be shooting at another man, but I felt obligated to go and defend our homes." Trace had a note of sadness to his voice as he spoke of his part in the

5

fighting.

"No problem; they were just Johnny Rebs anyway. We've spent about four years trying to kill them." The man just smiled as though he had enjoyed the killing.

"They were men fighting for what they believed in, and they were made by God; just like us Northerners. I sure hope I never have to shoot at another man."

"Son, it's a shame that all men don't feel that way. By the way, what are your names? If we're going to stop and get some of that good food, we should be able to tell them who sent us."

"Carrie Johnston and Trace Williams. And yours?"

"Oh, I just go by Donovan and that's Taggart." Taggart just nodded, as he was named by Donavan.

"You fellas better hurry to catch them before Carrie's folks pick them up and they leave. They'll be able to give you more for your trip than just sharing what they have for the social."

"Sure nice to meet such friendly people."

"Where out west are you fellas heading?"

"Once we hit St. Louis, then we'll make up our minds."

"The best of luck to you, a lot of places to pick from. What kind of work are you planning on doing?"

"Anything to make a living." It was the first that Taggart had spoken.

"You'd better get a move on and get some food in you." Trace started the team towards town as the strangers rode off towards the farm and the west.

Harry and Sara were hurrying to get started to pick up the Williams. Harry was calling to Sara to hurry, saying they were running late. She did some last minute packing of the food baskets and placed them in the back of the wagon.

"Sally and Tom are going to be waiting for us. You know Tom; he's always on time."

"And Tom knows I'm always late," replied Sara with a laugh.

Traveling down the road a few miles they noticed some strangers coming their way. Seeing the strangers had stopped, Harry pulled the team to a stop.

"Hi, neighbor, sure is beautiful country out this way," Donavan gave a big smile as he tipped his hat to Sara.

"It sure is; are you moving to this area?" Harry inquired.

"No, what makes you ask?" was Donavan reply.

"Well, you said neighbor, so I assumed that it meant you lived close by." Harry had an uneasy feeling about the two men.

"Harry, isn't that Tom's …"

"We've got to be going. We're running late. You two have a good trip," Harry said as he pushed the team on down the road. Hoping not to be stopped by the strangers.

"Harry, do you have to drive so fast. I was just about to ask if that was Tom's horse that man was riding? You certainly weren't overly friendly to the strangers."

"No, I wasn't. And, yes, that was Tom's horse. I'm worried about how those strangers got him. Tom wouldn't sell him, and the other one had Trace's horse. I just hope Tom and Sally are ok." He had the horses running as fast as he safely could. "I couldn't say anything, I don't have a gun and they each had pistols and rifles. And I have you with me."

After a few fast miles down the road, Harry was pulling up to the front of the Williams' home. Harry hurriedly gave out a call for Tom. Receiving no response, he entered through the door to face what he had feared. Tom and Sally were both lying on the floor with a pool of blood around them.

"Don't come in, Sara. Please, don't come in." Harry left the house with tears in his eyes, finding it hard to get words to say to Sara. Sara and Sally were like sisters.
How would they tell Trace and Carrie? They would have to notify the sheriff when they got to town. Going on to town, they were heading the opposite way of the men Harry knew had done this. It was giving them more of a start on any posse.

Tom also knew they would have to make the funeral arrangements, as Trace would never have experienced anything like this. He knew they had to pull themselves together and get to town. They had to face Trace with the news.

Chapter Two

Life-changing News

Trace and Carrie were mingling among the young folks at the social; most everyone in the community knew each other. The church was the central meeting place for all.

"Where are the folks?" The minister asked of Carrie and Trace. "We were certainly expecting them today."

"They'll be along soon. They're coming together, Reverend. But, I'm wondering if it wasn't Ma's pies you were looking for?" Trace had a big grin as he teased the minister.

"Oh! Trace, that's an awful thing to say to the Reverend." Carrie blushed through a grin as she tugged on Trace's arm.

"Well, I must say I was looking forward to having some of Sister Sally's pies." The minister laughed as he slapped Trace on the shoulder.

"They should be here soon. I thought that they would have been here by now." Trace glanced towards the road as he commented to the minister. "They're bringing the food with them."

"Well, I'm sure they'll be here soon; your dad is never late."

"But remember, my folks are picking them up and my mother is always late." Carrie was laughing as they headed over to talk to a group of young people.

A few minutes later the Johnstons' wagon was seen coming down the road. The team was moving at a faster pace than Harry usually drove them. The way he pulled up and jumped off, almost forgetting Sara, drew a lot of attention.

Carrie, first noticing the arrival, grabbed at Trace's arm as he was busy talking to some of their friends. "Trace, something's wrong - where are your mom and dad? Why aren't they with my folks?"

A crowd was forming around Harry and Sara, but Harry just pushed through the crowd and called out, "Sheriff! Reverend!" That caused even more concern, as they saw the look of panic on the tear-stained faces of Harry and Sara.

"Right here, Harry, what's wrong?" The sheriff was trying to calm Harry down. "Some of you ladies take Sara and see to her. Reverend, he wants you too."

By this time, Trace and Carrie were with them. Trace was upset to see the looks on their faces; he knew something bad had to have happened. Carrie started to leave to be with her mother, but her dad took her arm. He thought it would be best for her to be with Trace when he broke the news to him.

"Trace, Carrie, there is no easy way to say this, but it must be said. Trace, your Mother and Dad are dead. They've been shot by two strangers that we met on the road. When we passed them and exchanged a few words, I noticed that they were on yours and your dad's horses. They were armed and I wasn't, and I had Sara with me.

When I got to your place, I found your mother and dad on the floor; both had been shot. I covered them and left right away to get to you and the sheriff. You have to know how sorry I am to tell you that." Tom was visibly shaken and hurt by the loss of his two best friends and having to tell of it to their son.

Trace fought to hold back any tears. Carrie put her arms around Trace to try and comfort him. The minister put his arm around Trace and suggested that he come and sit down for a while. The sheriff, taking Harry's arm, said they needed to talk. He would have to ride back to the farm and take some men and a wagon to bring Tom and Sally back. He would see about raising a posse, but there was little chance of catching the killers in the state. So they'd have to wire for a federal marshal. He suggested that Harry, if he was going back with Trace and the others, have a drink before starting.

Trace got the wagon ready for the ride back to the farm. Before he left, he saw a lawyer, Mr. Grayson, who was friends of both families.

"Mr. Grayson, I would appreciate it, if you would handle the farm and anything Ma and Pa had in the bank. I want to give Mr. Johnston complete control over everything. If I don't make it back, he can keep the farm or sell it, whatever he thinks best."

"What do you mean, if you don't make it back? Where are you planning on going? What are you going to do?" Carrie was upset over the deaths, but more upset over hearing Trace's statement to the attorney.

"I'm going after Donavan and Taggart. They'll pay for Ma and Pa's deaths. After I see Ma and Pa, I'm starting out after them. Your Pa will make sure they are

11

buried proper." Trace's words were slow and soft, but firm.

"Well, you can't go after them alone. The sheriff said he would get up a posse in the morning. You might as well wait on them." Carrie didn't really want Trace to go at all.

"You know giving over the rights to bank accounts and title to the farm are big steps to take and I would advise against it." Mr. Grayson felt he should advise Trace that giving such authority to anyone was not wise.

"I'd trust Carrie's folks the same as I would my own, so would Ma and Pa. I'm going to ask Mr. Johnston to lend me some money to start out on, and I want him to be able to get it out of the bank. I want to get started right away. So, please, just write it down quickly for me to sign." Trace had made up his mind and wanted to move right away to get on the trail.

Harry brought Sara back with him. He felt she'd be better off at home and with Carrie. Carrie rode with Trace. Even though others thought they should drive his wagon, he insisted on driving home himself. The sheriff, minister, Mr. Grayson and some others rode along with them.

The trip was a sad and quiet one - one of deep hurt. The trip took only an hour, but it seemed like an eternity to get there. Harry asked Carrie not to go in, but Carrie wanted to be with Trace and not leave him alone to face the tragedy that laid before him.

The site brought tears to Trace's eyes. As much as he fought, he couldn't hold back the tears. After a few minutes, Harry took Trace by the arm and led him out so the men could load Sally and Tom on the wagon to take them to town to prepare them for burial.

Trace walked Carrie to her dad's wagon and tried to say goodbye to her. Sara heard him say he would be leaving at first light to track down the killers.

"Trace, you are not staying here alone tonight. And you can't go after the men by yourself. They are much older and more experience than you. You'll only go off and get yourself killed. Your mother and dad wouldn't want that. You've got to think of yourself and think of Carrie. Now, you get in this wagon and come home with us. We will fix you a cot out by the fireplace and you and Harry can talk in the morning." Sara didn't want to see the boy whom she thought of as a son, the one who would surely be marrying her daughter soon, being left alone at a time like this.

"Well, ok, it will be closer down the road to start. But I'll just sleep in the barn tonight. Don't you go to any trouble. Let me get some of my gear and my guns." Trace had his mind made up to go after the men who did this to his folks and there would be no changing it.

"We'll have a good breakfast in the morning and then you and Harry can talk. I know you'll want to stay for the funeral." Sara thought she'd try to get Trace thinking and maybe be able to talk him out of going off by himself.

The ride to the Johnstons' farm was a quiet one. Nobody knew what to say. Grief had overtaken them all. They had so many plans for the future and so many good memories. All were ended by the two strangers. The men who Trace had told to stop at the house and his mother would see that they were fed. Now, Trace must find them and see that justice is done.

Arriving at the house, Trace started to unhitch the

team, but Harry told him to go on in the house and he would take care of the horses. Sara told Carrie to bring Trace in and she would put on a pot of coffee. Carrie had trouble looking at Trace - tears came to her as she felt his hurt.

Harry came in and joined them at the table. He said that the minister was arranging everything for the funeral. The sheriff was wiring for a US Marshal in case the two killers got out of the state before the posse could catch up with them. It was best for Trace to let the law handle it. After the funeral they would have plenty of time to talk over how was best to handle the farms.

Trace, with his head still hung low, answered slowly, "I'll be leaving at first light to find them."

"Trace, you have to stay for the funeral. You can't just leave and not be there for it. Besides, the sheriff and the posse won't be here at first light. So get it out of your head about going after them by yourself." Harry was talking to Trace as he would to his own son.

"I'll appreciate you looking out for things for me while I'm gone, and I'd appreciate you lending me some money tonight. I'll be leaving at first light. Mr. Grayson has a paper for you to get the money out of the bank. Also, if anything happens that I don't make it back, the farm is yours to do with whatever you want." Trace stood up to leave. "I had better head out to the barn to try to get some sleep. I'll be riding hard in the morning."

"You mean you won't be staying for your father and mother's funeral? I can't believe it." Sara was shocked.

"I can't do them any good here. I have to get the men who did it. That means getting on their trail as soon as possible. No disrespect meant." Trace started leaving the house.

"I'll walk to the barn with you, Trace." Carrie was hurting over the loss, plus sharing Trace's hurt too. She wanted to be with him.

"You had better let him get some rest, honey." Sara was hard pressed trying to think of how she could best help Trace and Carrie.

Trace and Carrie hugged. They both knew it might be the last time for quite a while they would see each other.

With the lights out, Sara laid trying to sleep. Harry had finally drifted off; she could tell by his breathing. Sara heard the light squeaking of the side door. Slipping quietly to the window, she saw what she had feared. In the moonlight's soft glow was Carrie, with her shawl around her shoulders, on her way to the barn. Not knowing what to do, she did what most mothers would do - she knelt at her bedside.

In the morning, after chores, Harry came into the house for breakfast and gave them the news that Trace had left. The young man was off on an adventure like none he had ever known. Where or how long it would take, Trace had no idea. But he knew what he must do.

A couple of hours later, the sheriff and the posse rode up. The sheriff was upset that Trace had left on his own. He told Harry that he had a wire saying that these two were probably the same ones that had broken out of a Pennsylvania prison and had robbed and killed several people on their way across Ohio. These were not the kind of men that Trace was used to dealing with. Harry chose not to tell Sara or Carrie about it.

Chapter Three

The Trail of Vengeance

It was a bright crisp morning. It would be a good day for a ride under different circumstances. Trace knew the road well for the next forty or fifty miles, but after that he would have to be asking his way along. He didn't get as much sleep during the night as he had hoped for. But he was glad that Carrie came to spend time with him before he left. She gave him a tintype with her picture. She had bought it for his birthday but gave it to him to take along to remember her by. He loved the tintype, but he would've remembered her without it. She was in his heart, soul and mind forever. He was missing her already.

He knew the ride would be hard. Donavan and Taggart had a good head start. They probably rode hard till dark and found a place to hole up. They would know that it would be awhile before any posse started looking for them; so they would probably sleep and start the westward travel with the sun.

Trace realized he would need a lot of luck to catch up with them. Then, when he did find them, he needed a plan as to how to handle them. He had practiced his fast draw, as most kids have, but never thought he would really need to use it. Characters, in the different dime novels that he read, would say all different ways they used to be fast guns. Everyone tried to say something different. But all seemed to say that fast doesn't matter if you don't hit what you shoot at. At the speed he had practiced, he was accurate. But shooting old bottles was not the same as shooting at a man. The bottles had no way to shoot back. Both Taggart and Donavan showed they had no problem shooting at a person. When he caught up with them, he would have to be ready to take them, for they couldn't let him point them out to the law. Of course, he had no intention of that. He hoped that he could catch them one at a time. If they hadn't done anything in the town they were in, the town folk would think they were two friendly travelers not looking for trouble. He, himself, invited them to the church social and then told them to stop at his house and his mother would give them a good meal and food for travel. He had to remember that behind the friendly smile of Donavan was death.

It would be a different life out on the trail. He would be sleeping out in all kinds of weather. There'd be no family or friends around if he needed help or even for the company. And most of all, he wouldn't have Carrie. He knew she would always be there for him. Now he left her behind, not knowing when he would ever see her. He must clear his mind of all those thoughts and concentrate on what was ahead of him. He has to take good care of his horse for it has to last him till he takes his back from Donavan and Taggart; if those are their names. It was a thought that just occurred to him. His thoughts were coming too fast now. How would he describe the two killers to the people he would be asking if they had seen them? He knew the horses they were riding, if they hadn't stolen others already. They may have changed their clothes. They could have shaved. He needed to ride faster, but he had to watch that his horse didn't give out. He was sure that they would head to Evansville and then try to leave the state so that no posse could follow them. He wasn't a posse and he would follow them. It was hard not to think of Carrie, not knowing if and when he'd ever see her again. It was easy picturing her face. He had a tintype of her, but it wasn't the same as having her near and touching her. It would have to do for now. It was all he had.

Trace saw some tracks that left the road and headed down a hill to a clump of trees. Following them, he came to a place where he believed they had camped for the night. A trail leaving the campsite headed back on the road toward Evansville, so he thought he was on the right trail. He felt that they were a good six to eight hours ahead of him. He would have to take shorter rest breaks to pick up some time. After they crossed the state line, he believed they would think that no one would be following them. Or they might feel confident and spend some time in Evansville. He wasn't sure how much money they had taken from the farm. It certainly wasn't worth his mother and dad's lives.

Night came on fast, but Trace rode on for quite a while. The moonlight lit the road making it easy to follow at a pace that was not too hard on his horse. He felt as though he had traveled a good distance today. The wind coming down from the north felt like a late snow storm. The moon was going behind clouds at faster intervals, meaning the clouds were building into a storm. It was something he hadn't expected with Saturday being so nice and warm for the social. In a way, it seemed so long ago, although it was only yesterday. He started looking for a place to camp for the night where he would have some protection from the wind. Seeing a gathering of trees, he headed for them. With a stream running close by, it would be a good place to camp for the night. Finding a spot where a downed tree would offer a break from the wind, he started a fire to make some coffee and to take some of the chill off the night. While setting watching the fire grow lower, an old song started going through his mind.

THE CAMP FIRE'S BURNIN' LOW
AND THE AIR FEELS OF SNOW
IN MY HEART FIRES STILL BURN
AS MY THOUGHTS OF YOU RETURN
STILL YOUR PRESENCE LINGERS ON
THOUGH OUR DAYS TOGETHER'S GONE
I'M JUST A LONELY COWBOY
WITH A DREAM THAT RIDES ALONG
(DREAM THAT RIDES ALONG)

With Carrie on his mind, he spread his blanket to wrap around him and laid his head on his saddle to fall asleep from the stress of the day. The tears ran down his cheeks; the loneliness and the hurt of his loss were hard to bear. He took the tintype of Carrie from his pocket. Holding it so the firelight showed her face in the picture, he finally fell asleep.

Chapter Four

A New Kind of Life

Being a farm boy, Trace was used to rising before the sun. He stirred up the fire and added a few more sticks of wood to heat up some coffee and warm a couple biscuits. It would be enough to get him started for another hard day on the trail. He had covered a lot of miles yesterday, so he should be coming on to Evansville in a day or so. He had no idea whether or not he would find Donovan and Taggart still in town.

Arriving in Evansville, he figured the one thing he could do was look for his horses. If they are here, there is a good chance that Donovan and Taggart are still here. As he rode over to the livery stable, he kept his eyes peeled along the street for the horses or maybe the men. He got off his horse and checked with the man working the livery stable about some oats for his horse. Trace, after a few words of friendly conversation, asked if any strangers had come to town in the last couple of days and was told that he was the first to be noticed. Trace thought the saloon would be the best place to look.

Trace was not used to saloons, but he would have to get used to them. Donovan and Taggart probably frequented them often. Walking in carefully, still not sure how to call the play should the two be there, he took a seat at a table near the wall. A girl came to his table with a big smile and asked what he'd be having.

"Could I have a sandwich and a glass of water, please?" Trace felt as out of place as a skunk at a social.

"Usually people stop down at the restaurant for that, but I'll see what I can do for you." She smiled at Trace knowing he must be a farm boy. "Are you new in this area?"

"Just passing through. You didn't by chance see a couple other strangers passing through in the last few days?" Trace tried not to be too obvious.

"A couple of men came by earlier. The sheriff didn't like their looks, so he told them to keep travelin'. They didn't put up much of an argument about it. Of course, the sheriff had a shotgun and a couple of the local people backing him up."

"Did you notice which way they headed?"

"No. Now what's a nice boy like you wanting to ride with those kind of guys? The sheriff is a pretty good judge of character, and he ran them out of town right off. Why don't you go home and stay out of trouble." The girl seemed to have a sense of concern for Trace, probably because of his manners and way of speaking.

"Well, I appreciate your warning, but I don't want to ride with them. And I wasn't a good judge of character when I met them before, but I know what they are like now. I think I'll go talk to the sheriff."

"You don't have to look for him; he's been watching you for the last few minutes." She motioned for the sheriff as she went to get Trace his glass of water and to find him something to eat.

"Hello, young man, what are your plans here in our fair town?" The sheriff talked polite, but there was no mistaking he took his job seriously. "Passing through or planning on staying around awhile?"

"Just passing through, but I would like to ask a question of you."

"Ask."

"The two men you talked to this morning - do you know which way they're headed? I'm trying to find them."

"What do you want to get mixed up with those two no-goods for? You'll only end up in trouble, if you're not already in trouble. I ran them out as soon as I saw them. It's a wonder they haven't been shot or hung yet. I know them from a ways back. When we were in the army, they were always in trouble for stealing or cheating at cards." The sheriff was a plain talking man, and said exactly what he thought.

"I don't want to mix with them; I plan on killing them." Trace figured the sheriff was plain talking, so he thought he might as well be, too.

"I guess you got a grudge against them for something, but you killing those two won't be easy. They're as sneaky and deadly as a fox in a hen house. Just why and how do you plan to accomplish this task of yours?" The sheriff was a little taken aback at Trace's statement.

"I'm not sure how. It depends on where I find them and if they are together. But I'll find a way. They killed my folks a few days back. So, one way or another, I'll get them."

"I'm sorry to hear about your folks, but you being angry don't give you the right to take the law in your own hands. If you do it in my town and it's not a fair fight, I'll hang you. Now that's for sure."

Trace didn't doubt the sheriff at all; he was sure the sheriff meant what he said.

"Son, you are kind of young to be out on your own after two like that. Go back to the law in your town, give them the description of Davis and Tate and let the law send out posters on them. Don't ruin your life or maybe lose it. It's hard to tell how long it will take you to find them. You got to eat, sleep someplace, and feed your horse. You may end up living like they do, stealing and killing. Do you want to live that kind of life?" The sheriff paused and looked at Trace. "I can tell you've been raised to live a different kind of life than that."

"I noticed you call them Davis and Tate. They gave me the names of Donavan and Taggart when I met them." Trace tried to change the conversation.

"They probably change their names a lot more often than they do their clothes. You say you met them?"

"They were on the road leading to our farm. My girl and I were heading to a church social. They asked directions. I told them to stop at our place to get something to eat and my Ma would fix them up some food to travel on. I told them to go to our place, and for it, they shot my dad and mother." Trace started to get tears in his eyes, so he turned his head as though looking around for something.

"Son, you can't blame yourself for what happened. Do as I say, go home. Even if you find them and kill them, your life will change. You said you have a girl. By the time you find them and, if you do make it back home, she may have found someone else. Who's taking care of the farm for you? Anybody?"

"I signed it over to Carrie's dad, the farm and the

bank account. They had the farm next to us and were best friends with my folks."

"Take my advice and go back to your farm and live your life; your folks would want you to."

"I appreciate your thoughtfulness, but my mind's made up. I'm going after them." Nothing or no one could change Trace's mind.

"Well, good luck; just watch Tate, or Taggart as you called him. He has a sleeve gun and probably a derringer in his boot. Davis, Donavan or whatever he's going by, will have a lot of friends. People like that big friendly smile of his and will believe him. If they really don't know him; well, they won't believe you. And both of them are good with guns; handgun or rifle, they're good. They headed west, probably getting out of the state since they killed your family and no telling who else. They'll probably be found in some saloon; they like the cards and women. Better eat that sandwich Angel made you, and instead of just drinking water, learn to drink a beer. It won't draw attention to you as much as just asking for water. Just don't drink too much of it. You'll need a clear head at all times." Pausing for a minute, he looked at the waitress, "Angel, put his meal on my tab." The sheriff shook Trace's hand and left with a heavy sigh.

Trace headed for the livery stable to pick up his horse and get back on the trail. The temperature had definitely dropped and the gray clouds made it look like he would hit snow as he kept moving west. He wasn't sure how soon he would hit another town. It was certain that Donavon and Taggart were heading west just like they said. So his best bet would be to head for St. Louis. It's a big town and surely they would want to stay there for a while and get the feel of the west and find where they would best be able to apply their trade.

Trace had been heading west, just following the road, for a couple of days now. The weather turning cold so fast was an unpleasant surprise. The wind had little resistance in this flat land with low rolling hills. As the snow started flying it looked like it was turning into a blizzard. He had heard of these early spring storms and of travelers getting stranded. People who were not used to living off the land, sometimes didn't make it.

Trace spotted a buck upon a hillside. The snow was falling heavier and he needed a place to hole up till the storm passed. The buck would be a bargain card for him to play in trying to get someone to let him sleep in their barn and maybe get a good home-cooked meal. With one shot he downed the buck. Now he had to get up the hill to the deer and drag it back down. With the snow falling heavier, that would be a job in itself. Then, throwing it over his horse and finding a place to offer the buck in exchange for a place to sleep would be another job. The way the snow was falling and with night coming on, he hoped it would be soon. After riding a few miles, he saw some lights a little back from the road. The farmhouse was setting out here in a lonely part of the country.

Trace's New Family

Riding up to the little farmhouse, Trace hollered out, "Hello inside." Then he waited for a response.

The door opened slightly, and a voice responded, "Who are ya? What do ya want?" the voice sounded of one who had age.

"I'm looking for a place to get out of the storm. I have a deer here that I'm more than willing to share for some food and being allowed to sleep in the barn."

"Come up closer where I can get a look at ya." The door opened a little wider and Trace could see a shotgun part way out of the door. Trace got off his horse and led him up closer to the house. Tying his horse to the hitching post, he took off his hat and walked closer to the door. The man, seeing Trace's youth and the deer on the horse, opened the door and said for him to come on in.

Trace saw the man was up in years and leaning on a homemade crutch. His wife, standing over by the fireplace, smiled at Trace as he entered.

"Come over to the fire and get warm, and I'll pour you a coffee and fix up something for you to eat." The woman looked frail. "We haven't got much, but we'll share with anyone who needs some help."

"I would appreciate the coffee right now, but I would like to put my horse in the barn. Would you be interested in some of the deer meat? I can only take a small amount with me, and if you can use it, I'll do the best I can at butchering it so you can prepare it the way you see best." Trace saw that neither of them was really able to dress the deer. As tired as he was, he saw they needed some help. There wasn't much firewood stacked against the house. This late storm wasn't going to help them much.

After hanging the deer in the barn and bedding down his horse, Trace went back to the house to get something to eat himself. The cold Canadian winds were blowing the snow around as though it was January and not mid-April. He picked up some more firewood and carried it in as he entered the house. The old man commented that he was planning on bringing that in - in the morning. As Trace threw a couple logs on the fire to warm up the house, the old man said, "not too many, son, we don't like it too hot." Trace just said, "Yes, Sir," knowing the man was trying to make the firewood last.

"If you have an axe handy, I'll cut some more firewood before I leave in the morning. I'll try to help pay you some for your hospitality."

"Well, son, we'd be obliged, but it's not necessary. We try to help out when we can." The look on the old man's face showed that he would really like the firewood cut.

"The barn door is working kinda hard. I think I can fix that hinge so it will open and close a little easier."

"It's needed fixin' for some time now; Pa just hasn't been able to do much since he hurt his leg."

"I'll take care of it before I leave tomorrow. I do have to leave as soon as I can, but if there is anything that I can do to help you, let me know." Trace knew he needed to get on the trail as soon as possible, but he knew his mother and dad would have wanted him to help these nice people who were having a hard time of it.

After eating the food prepared for him and having some conversation with the two, Trace said, "I'd better head out to barn and get some sleep; it's been a long day"

"There's no need to go sleep in the barn. We have a roll up mattress Ma made. We can put it down by the fire for you. If our son had lived, I believe he would be about your age. Twenty or twenty-one?

"No, I'll soon be eighteen; I'm just a little big for my age." Trace found himself kinda blushing for some reason.

"I would like to think that our boy would have been like you; your mother and dad must be very proud of you." The lady had her hands on Trace's arm bringing him over to the fireplace.

"They're gone now." Trace started to get choked up. He took the mattress and laid it on the floor. He was handed a blanket as the couple went in the back room to go to sleep.

"Goodnight and thank you"

"Goodnight, Son, rest easy. By the way, I'm Sam Whitlock and my wife here is Nelly."

"Goodnight again, Mr. and Mrs. Whitlock."

The next day of helping turned in to three days. Saying goodbye to the Whitlocks was hard because they were so nice and needed help so badly. Trace wanted to get on the trail. He could stop in Marion and get some supplies sent out for the Whitlocks, but he should head straight for St. Louis now. He was low on cash; he would soon need some work to earn some money. Mr. Johnston didn't have much cash on hand to lend to him before he left. Still, these people needed someone to help them.

The town of Marion was not very large. Trace thought he'd look for the preacher in the town and talk to him about helping the Whitlocks. After inquiring around, he found the preacher and gave him all the money he could spare to buy some supplies for Mr. and Mrs. Whitlock. He also told the preacher that the farm was too much for them to keep up. He suggested that it might be a good Christian thought to try to find them a place closer to town where they could have a small garden and raise some chickens. They could sell eggs and some of the chickens to raise money to live on. Mrs. Whitlock may be able to do some sewing to help them along. Trace's sincerity must have touched the preacher's heart. He said he would certainly try to do all he could to help. The preacher thought to himself, what a remarkable young man.

So Trace was now on his way to St. Louis. The weather was getting to feel like spring again. The winds coming down from Canada had died down and a southwest wind was warming the area again. It would make the ride to St. Louis much better, allowing he didn't hit too many swollen streams from the melting snow. As he was riding, he took out the tintype of Carrie and just looked at it for a while, then held it to his chest. He missed her terribly. He knew, in this lifetime, that he would never see his mother and dad again; but Carrie he knew was back home. It seemed so long since he had seen her, though it had only been a little over a week. How long could he go on without her being with him? His thoughts were that the sooner he caught up with the two, the sooner he could get home and be with Carrie. He spurred his horse on a little faster.

Chapter Five

Donavan and Taggart Make Plans

St. Louis was a growing town. People coming west found it the starting spot of their journey. Many stayed to get in on the business to be had from all the pioneers getting equipped for the trip west. Many stayed to make a fast dollar by taking advantage of the lack of knowledge the people had in the supplies they would need, and some just to see which ones seemed to be carrying money that they could get from them one way or another. It was also a riverboat town. It was a perfect spot for Donavan and Taggart to get started at making some money to head to another western location to make more money the easiest way possible.

"Don't go getting into any gun scrapes until I've had a chance to win some money. We don't want to be leaving this thriving metropolis without a bank roll. You hear?" Taggart seemed to be a little more cautious of gun play than Donavan.

Donavan with his big smile, replied, "You just make sure you win. I'll watch for any big winner walking away from the tables who might like to share their winnings." Donavan laughed, "It's something the way people will go to such extents instead of makin' an honest livin', like robbin' banks and such."

"Yeah, I know how they will share with you; just don't start any trouble for us just yet. Let's get something to eat and get some of this dirt off of us, then find the right spot for me to work my profession." Taggart walked off heading for a restaurant, Donavan just laughed and followed.

After having dinner and getting a room and bath, Taggart headed for the High Times Saloon to look for a game. Donavan waited awhile in the room, so it wouldn't look like they were together. The High Times Saloon was crowded and loud, with girls hustling drinks and what Taggart was looking for, a couple of tables of card games. He looked over the tables at the men playing; trying to figure which would be the easiest to make some money.

Taggart went up to the bar and ordered a drink, "Place is kind of lively."

"Seems as long as we are open, people are here," the bartender remarked, as he wiped clean the spot at the bar where a couple men had just left. "New in town?"

"Yeah, I just got in today. Card games pretty much open to anyone?"

"Everyone's pretty much willing to take anybody's money. You see an empty seat, just ask if you can set in."

"I think I'll try my luck, thank you."

"Good luck."

"Gentlemen, mind if I set in?" Taggart asked in a friendly manner.

"The game is five card stud. If you like the game and got some money to lose, join us. The name is Carter. That's Jess, Andy and the young fellow there is Jake. We let him in the game because of his pretty sisters. We all know each other, but a new face is always welcome." Carter was the oldest of the players, a friendly, easy-going sort. "Thought I'd tell you we all knew each other so you wouldn't get the wrong idea if we say something to each other. Wouldn't want you to think you are in a rigged game of some kind. We just play for some fun."

"No problem, just looking for an honest, friendly game."

"Well, Jake's got shifty eyes, but he's honest." Carter's remark brought laugher from the other players.

"Maybe I need shifty eyes with Carter dealing," Jake said with a smirk. Again, the comment bought laugher from the men at the table.

The game lasted several hours and Taggart was only a few dollars ahead. He felt to try his fast hands with all friends in the game was a little too chancy. And it was a game for friends; no real money being bet.

"Well, Gentlemen, I think I'll try my luck at another game. Enjoyed your company." Taggart had noticed Donavan at the bar.

"Carter's a lawyer; he seems to carry the most money. I was only twenty to thirty dollars ahead. It was just a friend's game; no chance to make much from it." Taggart quietly spoke to Donavan.

"You're not such a great card player when you're not cheating, are you?" Donavan laughed.

"Oh, you're really funny, Donavan."

"So, you're new in town, too," Donavan said in a voice loud enough for the bartender to hear. "I just got in today. Busy town, isn't it?"

"Quite so, let me buy you a drink."

"Sounds good - always like someone else paying."

Donavan laughed as he accepted the drink.

With voices lowered, Donavan said, "I hear Abilene is a good town to head to.

"Need money to go there." Taggart was still looking over the room for a better card game.

"We can sell the horses and take a stage, or I noticed at least three banks in town. In fact, one's on the edge of town. Horses will be rested. It could be easy."

"Yeah, easy like the one in Indiana or the farm house."

"Well, it got us this far." Donavan was justifying his actions.

"Let me see if I can win some tonight. We still might take a bank, depends on what kind of luck I have tonight."

"Nice meeting you," Donavan said, turning to head back to his room to get some rest. They would probably be doing some hard riding if they took one of the banks tomorrow. He left Taggart continuing to try his luck.

His rest didn't last long because of gunshots being fired somewhere in the area. Figuring it might be Taggart getting caught pulling an ace from his sleeve, he grabbed their saddle bags and headed for the saloon. He was right on the money with what he had thought. Taggart was caught cheating. One of the men at the table went for his gun, but wasn't as fast as Taggart's sleeve gun. As Donavan got to the street, he saw a police officer taking Taggart off to jail. This really made a change in their plans. Donavan scanned the street looking for a couple of good horses that were saddled and handy. He had to watch and not get caught taking the horses till he could spring Taggart from the police. The two horses he picked were on the opposite side of the street from Taggart and the police officer. He wouldn't cross over till he was close to them. To make matters worse another officer joined the officer that had Taggart. Crossing the street quietly, he led the horses between him and the sidewalk. Stepping out ahead of the horses, he fired several shots hitting the police officers in the back. As they fell to the sidewalk, Donavan swung into the saddle of the one horse while pulling the other to the spot where Taggart could jump on the horse. They headed down the street, working their way out of town. St. Louis didn't pan out the way they had hoped. Now they were on their way to Abilene.

Country Boy in the Big City

It took Trace longer to get to St. Louis than he had planned. He was tired and hungry as he got into town. It was a lot bigger than any place he had ever been. The horse cars on rails in the streets were something he had never seen. Seeing a restaurant's bright lighting made him realize just how hungry he was. Checking the money he had left, wanting to be sure he had enough left to get a meal, he found it had better be a small lunch. He would have to clean up at the stable and sleep with his horse, that is, if the man at the stable would let him. He was going to have to find some work whether or not he found Donavan and Taggart. Even if he found them and lived through it, he would need money to get home on. He didn't want to end up doing what the sheriff in Evanston said might happen. He didn't want any parts of stealing or killing, except Donavan and Taggart.

He found the restaurant different than the small-town ones he had been finding on his way here. The prices were different, too. The waitress, who came to take his order, noticed the way he was looking at everything about the restaurant.

"First time to St. Louis?" She began to make small talk while placing a napkin and silverware at his place. She was trying to make him feel more at ease.

"Yes, just got in. That's why I have so much trail dust on me yet." Trace felt he must be a sight compared to the other customers in the restaurant.

"The special is a real good deal. It's a good price and fills you up real good. Plus your dessert comes with it." She smiled figuring Trace was probably low on money.

"Thank you, Miss. I think that's what I'll have." Trace blushed as he tried to watch his speaking and not sound like a country bumpkin.

"Rylee's my name."

"Reilly, your folks must have been planning on a boy giving you that name"

"No. My name is spelled Rylee."

"That's a pretty name for a pretty girl. Is your family from St. Louis?"

"My folks have gone their separate ways, but my brother and my sisters live here. That pretty girl over there is my little sister, Sofia. My older sister, Amber, is married. She and her husband own a hardware store on the other side of town. My brother, Jacob, everyone calls him Jake, works at the express office. If you're here long, you'll meet him, seems everyone does. Especially the girls. His big smile and beautiful blue eyes wins everybody's heart." She beamed with pride of her family.

"It's nice to have family; it means a lot."

"Let me see about getting you some food and coffee. It was nice talking to you. If you need help finding your way around, I'll help you the best I can." Rylee left to get his food giving him a big smile.

In a short time, Rylee brought Trace his meal. He thought it wouldn't be much use in asking, but he would try anyway. "I'm looking for a couple of men. I doubt if you would have met them. Their names are Donavan and Taggart."

The hearing of the names that Trace asked about made Rylee's expression change to a shocked look. Trace noticed the change in her looks right away.

"You heard of them? Are they here in town?" Trace felt the excitement in his whole body at the thoughts of finally catching up with the men he would have to face down.

Rylee walked away without saying anything. She couldn't believe that this nice young man was associated with two killers.

Sofia, seeing Rylee leave upset, came over to Trace's table and said, "What did you say to upset my sister?"

Trace, not knowing what was happening, was taken by surprise. "I don't know. I asked her if she knew a couple men and she got this look on her face and left."

"Who were the men?" Sofia was trying to figure out what had happened.

"Donavan and Taggart."

"My brother, Jake, was in a card game for a while with Taggart the other night. Then Taggart went to the bar and had a drink with a guy. People in the bar feel it was Donavan. Later, he got in another game and got caught cheating. He killed Sam Watts. While the police were taking him to jail, his partner shot two policemen in the back. They rode out of town kind of quick, so we don't know where '*your friends*' are."

"They're not my friends. I've been on their trail from Indiana. When I catch them, I plan on killing them. They killed my folks."

"I'm sorry; I didn't know. I don't know if the police have any idea where they were headed or not. But you had better be careful going after those two." Sofia realized that the two men he was after had no problems with killing.

Trace finished the meal although the news ruined his appetite. He didn't know when he would be able to afford another meal if he didn't get some kind of work. First, he thought he should see the police and see if they had any ideas where Donavan and Taggart were headed. The police weren't much help. By the time a posse was raised and because of the late hour of the night, there was no trail to be found. Posters were being printed up and sent to various towns. Out here, and especially further west, it was hard to track down some people without the luck of bounty hunters tracking them down. The police gave Trace the same advice as others - go home and let the law handle it.

So, it was another town that Trace has missed catching up with the killer pair. Trace knew he had to earn some money to live on until he caught up with Donavan and Taggart. He thought they would have been further ahead of him after he had stayed to help the Whitlocks. The thought came to him to look up the girls' brother, Jake, and see if he could help him find some work.

Finding the express office was easy and finding Jake was just as easy. The young man in the express office was talking and joking around with the other workers and the customers. It was easy to see why the girls were so proud of him; he certainly had a great personality. As he walked up to Jake to introduce himself, he was surprised as Jake called him by name. Reaching out to shake hands with Trace, he said, "It's not that big a town, and you met my sisters. They spread the news faster than the newspaper. How can I help you?"

"I guess I do look like I need help. I hope you know where I might get some work. I need to earn some traveling money." Trace noticed Jake looking at the colt hanging from his hip.

"You know how to use that gun? Jake was surprised that someone from the east would be carrying a gun in that manner.

"I grew up on a farm and I did a lot of hunting. I'm a pretty accurate shot, but I'm not looking to use a gun to make a living." Trace wanted it understood that he wasn't like Donavan and Taggart. He also realized as he answered that you didn't carry a holstered gun to go hunting.

"They're looking for an express rider to ride guard on the stage going to Abilene after stops in other small towns. It might work out good for you. That may be where Taggart and his buddy went. You can make some money and not have to spend it on traveling. You say you don't plan on using the gun to make a living. Out here and further west, you wearing your gun like that - you'll start. You look like you're looking for a gun fight, and there are lots out here to accommodate you. Mark my word; you'll be using it." Jake was only a few years older than Trace, but spoke with wisdom. "Come on, I'll take you to the boss."

The meeting with the manager of the express office

went well for Trace. The introduction that Jake gave and the sincerity of Trace convinced the manager that Trace was a responsible young man, one who could be trusted to do the job of guarding express shipments in between the towns that were not connected by the railroads. He had been told of the danger involved in these areas. Bandits believed to be ex-Quantrill raiders were robbing banks and shipments on a frequent basis. They were thought to be the Reno brothers and the James and the Younger brothers. Trace took the job to earn some money and to travel to different towns to locate the two that, so far, had eluded him. On taking the job, he knew he was obligated to do his best to protect the passengers, the money and freight being hauled on the stages.

Jake then offered to take Trace to his and his sisters' house and let Trace clean up and rest till he had to leave on his first run. As they walked down the street, Jake told Trace he would tell the girls that he was at the house, so they would let him sleep as long as he could. Jake laughed, "They'll feed you, too. They're like that."

The walk was suddenly interrupted as a stranger bumped into Trace; knocking him aside. It caught Trace off guard, not knowing what was happening.

"Sorry, Sir, I didn't notice you coming." Trace was being as polite as anyone could be, but the stranger was not looking for polite.

"I think you bumped into me on purpose, boy." The stranger spoke in a manner as to provoke a fight.

"I really think you bumped into me, but I still apologize to you, Sir." Trace tried to show he was not looking for trouble.

"Hearin' how you plan on killing two men that killed

a man and shot two police officers, I really expected you to have a little more sand. But, I did hear how you had a glass of milk at the restaurant." The stranger had a sarcastic grin on his face as he taunted Trace. "You're wearin' that gun tied down as though you know how to use it. Why don't we see just how good you are with it?"

Knowing he was being called out, Trace replied, "I told you, I'm not looking for trouble."

Jake spoke up, "Why don't you leave him alone; he apologized, leave it drop."

"Sonny, if you're going to talk, you better put on a gun, too."

"Most everybody in town knows me, and they know I don't start fights and I don't use a gun. If I have to fight; I'll use my fists against any man who would force it with me. So, if it's a fight you want, take off your guns and hang them over the railing, and we can get at it." Jake didn't plan on being drawn into a gun fight, but he didn't plan on running from any man who was forcing a fight.

"I don't plan on taking my gun off. I plan on using it against this little coward here." The stranger let it be known that he left only one way.

"Jake, stay out of it. Go over to the restaurant; I'm ok." Trace didn't want to see Jake get involved with his problem.

"There are two of them, Trace. I won't leave you." Jake showed that although he was known for his friendly, joking ways, he wasn't a coward.

"No, Jake. You leave now. I can tell that he's leaving no other way to settle this. I see in him what I should have seen in Donavan and Taggart when I met them. Go across the street -- NOW!" Trace's voice had changed; he had taken charge of the situation and knew he had no choice but to handle it.

As Jake walked away, Trace unlatched his Colt. He knew this is what it would be like when he met his two foes. He needed to stay calm, and he knew he had to be fast, but accurate. He knew where he had to hit this man and finish it with one shot. If he missed the first time, he would probably not have a chance for a second shot. Several people had been listening and stepped inside buildings to be out of the line of fire that they knew was coming.

The stranger, removing the cigarette from his mouth, spoke as cold as death itself, "When the cigarette hits the street, you'd better be fast."

Trace had no intention of watching the cigarette; he was watching the stranger's eyes. The stranger's eyes seemed to show some fear as he saw that the eyes of Trace had no fear at all. As his hand went for his gun, he was on his way to his grave. The stranger's gun never cleared his holster. His eyes got bigger as he felt the hot burning sensation in the center of his chest. As his knees started to sag, he dropped his gun as both hands went for his chest. The gunfight was over. Out of instinct, Trace had his gun on the other man that was with the dying gunman.

The man cried out, "Don't shoot, I'm not drawin', don't shoot."

The crowd started to gather around; a gunfight in St. Louis wasn't that common any more. Trace was still shaking from the whole affair.

A voice sounded from behind him making him turn quickly. "Take it easy, young fellow. We're gonna be working together. I'm glad to see that they hired someone that can handle himself." The voice was that of Stan Hollister, the man who would be driving the stage that

Trace would be riding guard on.

Trace still couldn't find words to say. He had shot at men during Morgan's Raid. But then he was not shooting by himself and at a man just a few feet from him. He felt a hand on his shoulder that made him jump. He turned to see Jake. Jake said something to Hollister and then said for Trace to come with him.

When the police arrived on the scene of the shooting, Stan explained what had happened. He told them that Trace worked for the express company now and Jake was with him when the men approached him and started the fight. "He had no other way out. I was right behind him when the man started to draw his gun. He had his hand on his gun before Trace made his move. The man just wasn't quick enough or it would have been Trace lying there on the street."

Jake walked Trace down the street to his house. Trace had not yet said anything. It was an experience that he didn't enjoy, and it left him not knowing what to do or say. Jake kept his hand on his arm as they walked down the street. Jake's words came back to haunt Trace, "Out here, if you wear your gun tied down like that, you will find you have to use it." A sick feeling came over Trace. He knew he had to adjust. This is the way life will be out here.

"I have to get back to work. Stan will knock for you when he's ready to leave. I wish you luck." Starting to leave, he turned saying, "There's something I thought of that might help you if you meet up with Taggart. I was in the saloon the night he shot Sam Watts. Watch him; he carries a sleeve gun. It's his left sleeve. I think it's on a spring because it was in his hand before Sam could clear his holster. I think Sam was watching his right hand."

Then he added, "Get some sleep; you couldn't help what happened here. He was asking for it."

Trace was tired and it had been a long day. Upset as he was, the bed felt good. He soon fell asleep wondering how many towns and incidents like tonight laid before him.

Chapter Six

The Start of a New Job

Stan Hollister's banging on the door finally woke Trace. The sleep definitely wasn't enough but did help. Getting up from the bed, he took the picture of Carrie that was lying on the pillow and put it in his shirt pocket. He glanced at it again, while hurrying to answer the door. Seeing it was Stan, he knew he was at the start of a new adventure. One that would bring a lasting change to his life.

Trace had to go to the stable, get his gear and throw it on the top of the stage, and he was on his way at his new job. The strong box was loaded underneath the seat of the driver. Trace noticed that two shotguns were there, also. He placed his Henry on the top of the stage where he could easily reach it. Trace liked the Henry because it gave sixteen shots if needed. He put a shotgun across his legs because they said that's what most guards liked. Shotguns are great for close range, especially if you're not a good shot. Trace liked the comfort of knowing his Henry was in arms' reach of him. Stan checked the hookup of the team and the condition of the lines and the stage himself, although the fellows hooking it up were responsible for checking it. He prided himself with the safety of the trips he made. Then he checked that the passengers were accounted for and the luggage and doors secure. He gave a shout and snapped the whip above the team, and they were on their way.

Stan looked Trace over as they started down the street to head out of town and into the open country between here and the next town. "You'll notice out here some men wear two gun rigs. Not a bad idea if you're being chased by a gang of road agents or Indians are after ya. What I like is the side holster and a belly holster. I keep a thirty-eight in the belly holster; it's easier to draw and still has enough kick to do the job. Ya might want to pick one up; ya never know when it will come in handy. We'll be in some rough territories and yer looking for those two men, it could be awfully handy." Stan spit a mouthful of tobacco juice at a bush as they rode passed it.

The job was monotonous, hours of just riding. Stan was a nice enough man, just not much of a talker. It was hard just trying to keep your eyes peeled for any kind of trouble. After making a couple of stops at relay stations, Stan asked Trace, "Ya noticed the three men watering their horses?"

It was while they were stopped at a station for a change of team that Trace had noticed that the men acted as though they were just tired from riding. He didn't like the way they were looking over Stan, himself and the passengers. Trace commented, "I noticed." They left the relay station in the usual manner and continued their journey.

A few miles down the road, Trace saw a flash of light from trees along the road. The sun shining through the trees must have reflected on something metal. Pulling back the hammers on his ten gauge shotgun caused Stan to reach under his seat and put his shotgun across his knees.

"It's probably them. Swing wide of those trees and make them come out for us. They'd probably like to just bushwhack us from the trees." Trace was taking charge of the situation; it was the way his mind worked.

Stan, though older and more experienced, liked the idea. He swung over into the field hoping not to hit a rock or rut that would break a wheel. The plan worked and the three riders came out from the trees to give chase to the stage. Stan was headed back to pick up the road to make smoother travel. The passengers, being bounced and thrown about while going off the road and riding through the field, were hollering. The riders came on a shooting and trying to overtake the stage.

"I'm going on top. If they get alongside, try to get down in the boot. If they get me, throw the shotguns off and stop and give them the box." With that Trace climbed on top and laid flat with his Henry as he located the three riders.

Stan kept the pressure on the team to try to keep a distance between the stage and the three outlaws in pursuit. He heard the Henry's report and then a silence. He wondered - why ain't he shootin'? Then he heard it again as he heard the outlaws still shooting at them. Then, pretty quickly, the third time. Trace was sliding back down on the seat.

"Ya ok, boy? Did they get you?" Stan was worried about the condition his young partner was in.

"No, you can slow down now; no one's following you." Trace did not explain the reason that no one was following. Stan just glanced over, saw the young man's face, and knew that the outlaws had misjudged the risk in trying to take the stage.

After a few minutes, Trace spoke to Stan, "I asked Jake before I left town to tell people that my name was Johnny. He said he would talk to the girls and the express boss and explain to them why I didn't want my real name used. I expect, after I find Donavan and Taggart, to go back to the farm and to get married. I don't want anything like what happened in St. Louis and here on the trail to be following me, as I try to live back home and work my farm. I hope to have a family soon, and I wouldn't want this life to turn up."

"No problem, Son; I mean Johnny. No problem at all."

As they put more miles behind them, Stan notice Johnny (he was thinking he had to remember to call him that) was looking at a tintype. Stan noticed that this seemed to relax Johnny, but gave him the look of a homesick or lovesick kid. He was one or the other or both. Stan finally asked, "Is that yer girl?"

"Yeah," he turned the picture for Stan to see.

"She sure is a pretty little thing." It was the end of the conversation for hours. But Johnny started humming, as a song ran through his head.

I LOOK AT AN OLD TINTYPE
I CARRIED FROM THAT DAY
IT'S BENT AND IT IS FADED,
BUT YOUR BEAUTY ALWAYS STAYS
THE PICTURE IN MY MIND
OF THE DAY WE SAID GOODBYE
IS THE PICTURE I WILL CARRY

UNTIL THE DAY I DIE
I'M JUST A LONELY COWBOY
WITH A DREAM THAT RIDES ALONG
          (DREAM THAT RIDES ALONG)

The rest of the trip was peaceful. The passengers asked Stan if anyone was hurt during the shooting; to which Stan answered, "Not that I saw."

One passenger that looked as though he traveled quite a bit commented to Stan, "That young man's going to be valuable to your company. When word spreads that there were three men and three shots is all it took, men will definitely think twice before trying to stop you."

Stan commented, "It would me."

The job and the traveling from town to town turned into months. The few times anyone tried to stop the stage, they met their death. Johnny's shooting was accurate and deadly. He did his job and his reputation grew. But still there was no sign of the pair that he was looking for.

Johnny mainly stayed to himself between runs. Anywhere he went, people would look, and he would hear comments like "That's him; I hear he's killed twenty-some men." People would step aside as he walked by, and the women would mainly go indoors when they saw him. As Trace, he was known for his easy-going, gentle ways. As Johnny, he was given the respect of a fast gun.

Johnny Makes Some New Friends (And Finds His Foes)

Then one day it happened; something he had never

faced. A young man was in the middle of the street for a showdown with two men. What the young man didn't know was that on each side of the street behind him were men standing behind the corners to make sure the two in front of him came out alive. Johnny walked out to the middle of the street to the man (he later found out his name was Joe Rollins). Rollins, who wasn't expecting any help was getting a little nervous, with two men in front and now one coming from the side.

"That's far enough. One more step and you go down before these two." Rollins said, knowing it was a tight situation even for him.

"Just comin' to get your back. There are two in alleys behind you." Johnny kept coming.

Joe looked at the two in front of him. "I should've known that even with both of you coming at me, those other two pieces of dirt would be trying to back shoot me. You called your play now make your move or I will." Joe Rollins let it be known that Jim Farrell and Whitey More had no choice now. Fear was seen in their eyes, but they had to make their move.

In the matter of a few seconds, both men laid dead on the dusty street. They had planned that Rollins would be back shot before he had time to draw. Instead, the two in the alleys moved back in and down the alleys. Realizing that it was Johnny they would be up against, they thought better.

Joe Rollins held out his hand to Johnny. "I owe you and I won't forget. I'm sure that someday, someway, we'll meet again. It's good to know that there is still honor left in the world today." Looking at the men lying in the street, he said, "Let the sheriff and his men handle this mess. They were watching and saw what happened. It would have been nice, if they had tried to warn me of the two behind me."

Walking towards the saloon, he commented, "Looks like a storm coming up." Rollins was talking fast like it was his nerves talking. "Can I buy you a drink? Come on, let's get inside. Here comes the rains." Rollins's talk showed that even a fast gun like him had nerves to deal with, too.

The saloon was busy, but not overly crowded. Most of the men in the saloon had just witnessed Joe Rollins gun down the two men in the street. Most had seen men shot before, so it was just another topic of conversation with them. They knew Rollins was fast and deadly, but what had their curiosity was, what was Johnny doing backing his play? Would these two soon be facing each other to see who would be the top gun? They seemed to be on friendly terms as they stopped at the bar.

After having a drink together, Rollins left for his room. Johnny was getting ready to leave when he glanced at the table in the corner. His heart started pounding; he could feel the cold sweat break out over his body. After months of searching, there was Taggart sitting in a card game. How should he approach this man he swore to kill? Should he call him to go out in the street? It was pouring rain out there. How about the men at the table with him? Were they friends of his? Where was Donavan? Were they still traveling together? These thoughts were racing through his mind. He knew it was what he had been searching for these past several months. He knew he had to call Taggart out and now was the time.

Flashing lightning and roaring thunder showed the rain had turned into a full-fledged storm. A man came in and broke his thoughts with a loud statement, "Those rains really brought a storm with them." Being a local man who frequented the saloon regularly, he thought nothing of how loud he was.

Johnny, while thinking, had been moving closer to the table. As he came up to the table, Taggart spoke up. "Care to join in? There's an empty chair."

Looking at Taggart with a deep burning hate, Johnny replied, "There'll be another one empty."

"Why? Is someone leaving with you?" Taggart did not recognize who was standing before him.

"Not with me. They'll be carrying you out after I kill you." The words Johnny spoke left no doubt he meant what he said.

"You know who you are planning on killing, Boy? I don't even know you."

"I know you, and I want to know where Donavan is. Have the man to your right, pick your watch up off the table. We'll see if I know what's engraved inside. If I do, you better be going for your gun."

"Pick up the watch, Sims; let's see if the young gunman there knows what's on the watch."

The man carefully picked up the watch and moved away from the table. The other men at the table slid their chairs back and moved quickly out of the way. Knowing that in a few minutes lead would be flying, they wanted to be out of harm's way.

As Johnny started saying, "To Tom, my love always, Sally," Taggart was rising up from his chair. He pushed his coat back with his right hand to leave his colt hanging clear at his side. As he raised his left hand, the derringer slipped into his hand. It was not fast enough as Johnny remembered Jake's warning of Taggart's left hand. The bullet from Johnny's forty-five at that distance drove Taggart back against his chair and over the side of the falling chair. The bullet hit his chest and was clearly through the heart of the fallen gambler. Johnny felt a burning sensation in his back and through the shoulder. As he heard the sound of another gun behind him, he realized he had probably found Donavan, also. This time he would not be taking on Donavan. The fact that he saw things get dark, as he was headed for the floor, proved that. The crowd gathered around, except for Donavan who was already out the door and heading for the nearest horse he could find.

Hearing the shots, Rollins came carefully down the stairs to find out what was going on. Was it someone else looking for him? A dealer said to Rollins that someone got his friend. Rollins pushed through the crowd and saw Johnny lying face down. The man who saved him from being back shot had been back shot himself. It looked like he might still be alive.

"Did someone send for the doctor?" Rollins wanted to help this new friend if he could. He was feeling guilty over not being there to help. "Some of you men help me get him up to my room. Careful with him."

"Good thing that one isn't your friend; he's as dead as last Thanksgiving's turkey. What your friend's name?"

"Johnny."

"Johnny what?"

"I don't know. I never heard a last name. The rains came and we came in and had a drink. I went upstairs and heard the storm start and then I heard the shots."

"Well, the rains came and a storm sure came for that

fellow. I think we might as well call him Johnny Rains, because the storm sure follows him."

"Come on; let's get him upstairs and get that doctor up there or we'll be calling him dead. And I don't want that. He's the only friend I have." Rollins had really taken a liking to this young man who put his life on the line for him. He planned to do everything he could to help him.

"Well, I think Johnny Rains is a good name for him and that's what I'll call him. You tell him when he wakes up." Others in the crowd nodded with approval as Johnny was being carried upstairs.

Johnny opened his eyes and found himself in a strange room. He could feel the pain in his back and shoulder and the feeling of the bandages around his chest and shoulder. Looking around the room, he spotted a young lady sitting reading a newspaper. He tried to move and the pain made him groan, drawing the attention of the young lady.

"Hi, you finally woke up?" She had a friendly smile as she came over to check on him. "So how do you feel, that is, aside from being shot?"

"I'm sorry. I didn't mean to disturb your reading."

"That's ok. It's two weeks old anyway. We don't have a paper here in town, so when someone has one, we all read it. Some of the people, I think, just look at the few pictures. Do you feel like something to eat?" The girl was fluffing the pillows in back of him as she talked. "You've been out of it for a couple of days, so I imagine you're pretty empty."

"Are you a nurse?" Johnny inquired, since the girl seemed to be taking charge of him.

"No, Joe just has me watching to make sure you're ok

and if you need anything." She handed Johnny a glass of water. "He's downstairs trying to win some money. Since he's been staying around town watching over you, he needs to make some money." She started walking to the door. "Let me go get you some soup; we'll start off with that for now."

"Wait a minute, how long have I been here? Did they get a description of the man who shot me? How long does the doctor expect me to lay here?" The questions came pouring out of Johnny.

"Well, one thing for sure, you got your wind back. You didn't take a breath through all those questions. You were out of it for about two days." She was young and pretty with long reddish-brown hair and dressed fancy. "Yes, they got a description and a name of the man that shot you. And you're gonna be laid up for probably three weeks to a month for that back and shoulder to heal. Now, I'm going to get you that soup. Relax."

"Before you go - what was the man's name?" Johnny wanted to know if his thoughts were right.

"Donavan."

"I figured it must have been him; I'd been looking for him and Taggart."

"You certainly found Taggart, but you're going to have to do some looking for Donavan. It will be awhile before you can do that." With a big smile, she said, "I'm going to get the soup." Then she left the room.

Johnny's thoughts went back to Carrie. He missed her more and more every day. It had been months now that he was following the pair. Now, it was down to one. How much longer would it be before he could return home? He had no word from Carrie. Did something happen to her? If so, why didn't her parents write? Was it that the letters weren't finding him? It was hard being away from her; they had been near each other since they were young kids. The thought of going back and his mother and father not being there was also hard. His life had already changed so much; a different name; men being killed; and how many more would challenge him or try to rob the stages or offices he was guarding. His friend, Joe, would be leaving once he saw that he was ok. Stan, he was sure, would have already left to make his runs. What was he to do until he could get on the trail of Donavan; and where would he even start to look?

Hunger started gnawing at his stomach. Where was that girl with the soup and who is she? He closed his eyes wondering when it all would end.

Chapter Seven

The Johnstons Have Problems

Carrie's life mainly consisted of looking westward hoping to see Trace coming back home. She found it hard to concentrate on anything else. While helping her mother around the house, she would be found just staring out the window or door, waiting. It had been over two months and no word from Trace. It seemed to her mother that the crying she would hear at nights was growing worse.

Mr. Johnston was trying to keep the two farms going. He had hired a couple of men to work between the two farms. He had told Sara that he didn't think Trace was going to make it back. If he was alive, they would have had some word from him. Sara kept hoping and praying that he would return. As she looked at Carrie, she prayed even harder. She had a feeling that Carrie really needed him to come home. She didn't want to question Carrie, but felt that soon, if Carrie didn't say something to her, she would have to ask. She was afraid if she asked, she would get an answer she didn't want to hear.

"Carrie, you can't go on this way. You will ruin your health. It's close to three months now and no word. You will have to face the fact that there is a chance Trace won't be coming home." Sara hated saying it to Carrie, but felt that she had to get on with her life. She did nothing but watch down the road hoping to see Trace riding back. She didn't want to go to town to see friends or even go to church.

"He has to come back soon, Ma; he just has to be back soon. He just can't be gone any longer. I need him back now." There was desperation in the way Carrie said it. The tears in her eyes told the story to Sara.

"You have a real problem; don't you dear?" Sara was choked up as she asked Carrie while putting her arms around her shoulders. "I'm your mother, do you think that I haven't noticed that you haven't had your time since before Trace left? I think we need to talk to your father."

"No, Mommy, not Daddy. He won't understand. He'll hate me. You know it wouldn't have happened if it wasn't for his parents getting killed and him leaving. You just can't tell Daddy." Carrie was desperately trying to avoid having her dad find out.

"We have to tell him; you'll soon be showing. He's got to know before someone says something. It's only fair to him." The look on Sara's face showed she was sharing the heartache with Carrie. She was also worried about how Harry would take the news. She knew he had to be told.

That night, when Harry came in from the fields, they had supper as usual. Harry couldn't help but notice that Carrie and Sara ate very little and talked even less. He knew that something was wrong.

After supper, he asked Sara, "What's wrong?"

Sara replied, "We have a problem." Sara's voice was breaking with each word as she hated to answer Harry.

Carrie just hung her head and sobbed. It didn't take

Harry long to realize the problem. He just looked at Carrie and then got up from the table, threw his napkin across his plate and walked into the living room. Carrie started crying and ran to her room. Sara followed Harry to the living room and put her arms around him. She knew the hurt he felt. Carrie was his pride and joy. She would always be his little girl. He was always so proud of her. He never would have expected this. And Trace, the son of his best friend, a boy he always loved like a son, and he did this. Him gone, most likely dead, and leaving Carrie like this. What is to happen now? Her reputation is ruined. In a small farming community like this, everybody knows everything and a baby born out-of-wedlock was not accepted for any reason. Harry broke down and cried. All Sara could do was hug him and tell him things would be alright. But she wondered, would they? They had to make plans as to what would be best to do.

The next morning, Harry just had coffee for breakfast and left to work in the fields. He said nothing to Carrie, not a word, a hug or a kiss as usual before going out. Carrie not only had the problem of carrying a baby, but now she felt hated by her father. Where was Trace? Why was there no word of him? Why would he leave her to face this alone? Sara knew her hurt and her fears and just gave her a shoulder to cry on. Carrie was her baby; she had problems and was hurt. Sara knew it would not have happened on either of their parts if it wasn't for the circumstances. But people, when they gossip, don't care for circumstances. What would Harry want to do? Would he want to send her away some place? She has never been away from home. Would he want to give the baby away to be adopted and raised by someone else? Just what was

Harry thinking?

The answer came soon. Harry came in from the fields in about an hour. He told Sara to start packing. He was going to town to see about selling the farms. They were moving and she wasn't to tell anyone about it. She wasn't to discuss it with Carrie and Carrie was not to tell anyone about moving or where they would go. In fact, she wouldn't know to tell anybody.

"I'm going to buy a wagon for the travel. We are heading west. As far as Carrie goes, her husband was killed in an accident with a horse. During our traveling, it happened. We'll try to hide our shame behind a lie." As Harry left to go to town, Sara saw Carrie standing behind the door. She had heard every word. As if things weren't bad enough, she heard how her dad thought of her. Carrie returned to her room to cry to herself, still praying Trace would return for her. She knew he would do right by her and stand by her all the way. But where was he?

The banker was surprised as Harry told him of his plans. Harry was well known, as was the rest of the family, and it was hard to believe that they would just up and sell the farms and leave. The question came up about the selling of the Williams's farm. Harry answered that if Trace were alive, they would have heard from him by now. When it was suggested that he take some time to think it over, Harry said that it was an opportunity he didn't want to pass up. He couldn't give any details at that time. He said the land office had both the deeds on hand, so there shouldn't be any problem. He needed some cash to handle getting ready for travel. The rest he wanted in a bank draft that he could deposit when they got to their new home.

Word spread quickly of the farms for sale. The minister heard and came to talk to Harry about his leaving. He asked if there was anything that he could do for the family. He was told "No, thanks." He asked if it had to do with the Williams's deaths, and Harry replied that things weren't the same. He shook hands with the preacher and left to buy a wagon. It was the last the preacher saw of Harry or any of the family.

It took a little more than a week to sell both the farms. It was prime land and easily sold. When Carrie heard that both farms were sold, she asked her dad how he could have sold Trace's land. Harry, coldly, told her that it was the least Trace could do after what he had done to her. He said that Trace owed it to her and the baby that he had left behind. He didn't want to hear another word about it. It was his and her fault that the farms had to be sold and they had to move. She asked where they were going and how would Trace know where to find her? Harry replied that he doubted Trace would ever be back, and if he did come back, he might shoot him himself. Carrie felt more lost and alone than ever. The only thing she had was a part of Trace in her and she would never give up their baby.

It was sad leaving the farms and friends and memories behind them. What laid ahead no one knew. The exact time and day the Johnstons left the area, no one was sure of. They left without a word to anyone. Only Harry knew where they were headed. Carrie kept looking back, wondering how Trace would ever find her. Her dad hardly spoke or even looked at her. She had no choice but to leave with them. She could never make it on her own. She knew her mother loved her and understood. It was the only thing that made her life bearable.

Harry crossed through Illinois and Iowa into northern Nebraska and there he bought some land to start another farm. This would be their new home. Carrie was to understand that there would be no contact with the people from Salem and the surrounding area. If she wanted a home for her and her child, she had to promise. Harry saw the hurt that Carrie was going through and it made him stop and think. He was hurt that his daughter was to be an unwed mother, but she was scared. Her whole world was turned upside down. The boy she was sure she would soon be married to was gone, and she was left expecting a child. She needed his love and understanding. He took her in his arms and told her that she was still his baby and always would be and that things would be alright.

Starting the new farm would be hard, but Harry could hire help. He had the money from the two farms plus the money from Trace's family's account. He felt no wrong in spending the money because the farm would someday belong to Carrie and the child that Trace had left behind. The soil was rich and should grow good crops. Wheat would be his biggest planting. With a railroad spur not too far away, he would be able to ship his crops to buyers without much trouble. He looked forward to a good life in their new home, and he actually found himself looking forward to having a grandchild. Sara was at peace, now that Harry had found his. This land and home could be a good life for them.

Chapter Eight

Johnny Leaves a Broken Heart

The weeks had really dragged along while Johnny was waiting for his body to heal. The girl, Stella, looked after him even after Joe had to leave. Johnny wanted to give her more money. She refused it, saying it was nice being around a gentleman after what she usually worked around. She asked Johnny, if he planned on staying around after he was well enough to take care of himself. He told her it would depend on whether the express company still had a job for him. If it did, it would mean his moving around. So, he wouldn't be settling in any certain place. Her face showed that she was upset at the thoughts of his leaving. With a slow nervous voice that was almost a whisper, she tried to explain to Johnny.

"You know, I don't do upstairs work here. I hustle drinks and sing. Mac, who owns the place, was a friend of my father's. When my father died, Mac took me in and gave me a job singing. He never tried to make me work upstairs. Most from around here know that, so I never get bothered that much about it." Looking at Johnny and trying to smile though hurting, she said, "I don't think you ever heard me sing, have you?"

"No, I haven't. But you have a beauty to your voice,

so I can imagine how you could be a singer. I had wondered why you were working here."

"My mother died when I was young, so it left my father to raise me. He did the best he could, but the years of hard work finally got to him. And as I said, Mac was his best friend; I believe they were kids together. So Mac took me under his wing. He's been really good to me. But I wanted you to know what I'm like; I didn't want you to think differently."

"Well, I think you're a very nice young lady, and I am very grateful for all the care you have given me. But, I have to keep moving on."

"Because of the picture?"

"Yes, I have to try and get back to her. I couldn't be happy without her. I'm afraid something is wrong. I haven't heard from her. But I would like to hear you sing before I leave."

"I'll sing a new song. I'll sing it just for you when you come down. And be careful and take it easy for a few days until you build up your strength. I'll see you downstairs." Stella left with tears in her eyes.

Stella was by the piano as Johnny came down the stairs. She spoke to Jimmy, the piano player, and he started playing softly. The room quieted down knowing Stella was about to sing.

I HEAR STRUMMING GUITARS
GAZE AT THE EVENING STARS
AS I HEAR SONGS OF LOVE
THE BIRDS SINGING ABOVE
EVERY SIGHT, EVERY SOUND
IN THE WORLD, ALL AROUND
EVERYTHING REMINDS ME OF YOU

ON A WINTRY DARK NIGHT
A SUMMER DAY SO BRIGHT
A BLOSSOM-FILLED MAY
COLORED LEAVES BLOWN AWAY
NO MATTER THE SEASON
YOU ARE ALWAYS THE REASON
EVERYTHING REMINDS ME OF YOU

THE SONGS OF LOVE THAT I HEAR
WORDS THAT SPEAK IT SO CLEAR
HOW CAN MY HEART POSSIBLY HIDE
WHAT I FEEL DEEP INSIDE
IT'S LOVE THAT IS TRUE
IT'S THE MAGIC OF YOU
EVERYTHING REMINDS ME OF YOU

The barroom was quiet as she finished. Then the applause was like Johnny had never heard in a barroom. Stella definitely had a beautiful voice.

"Stella, that was really beautiful."

"I'll never sing it again until I see you again." Stella had tears in her eyes as she slowly walked away.

It had been another three weeks and still no word from Carrie. He was worrying, thinking maybe something had happened to her. How far has Donavan traveled in the time he was in bed? He had sent word to the express office that he was able to go back to work. The express agent sent word for him to go to Breckenridge, Idaho, and guard the office. With a gold strike, they would be getting a lot of gold in the office and that was always a temptation to too many people in the area, and some from other areas. Plus, he thought it might be best for Johnny not to be bouncing around on the top of a stagecoach until he mended better.

Johnny had to say his goodbyes to the people who had helped him the past month. The hardest to say goodbye to was Stella, who was so good to him.

A New Job That Adds to the Legend

The ride to Breckenridge took several days. Upon arriving, he introduced himself to the agent at the office. The agent told Johnny that the gold was coming in fast and that he would be glad to get it on its way out of his care. Johnny looked the office over to see where would be the best places to take cover and get the best shots at anyone who would be trying to rob the office. If the office was robbed, it would probably be by several men. They would probably have one or two with the horses and at least one outside the door. Gold strikes always brought in the worst types. Two new saloons had just opened within the last couple of weeks. A wagon load of girls for the one saloon had just rolled in as Johnny arrived. It was a small town, mainly for the small ranches and farms that were getting started. Probably a lot of the farms and ranches were abandoned now that gold was discovered. Gold fever caught fast and spread fast. Johnny's thoughts drifted back to his farm in Indiana and how he wished he was there. The mountains of the Rockies were certainly different from the flat land of Indiana.

Days passed by and everything remained quiet. The stage that was to come to pick up the gold was late not by a few hours but by a couple of days. Johnny watched both day and night at who would be watching the office. He noticed that across the street several men seemed to linger to talk. And the same men, in different order, would watch when the express workers came, went to lunch and left for the day. Johnny got the feeling they knew why the stage was late and would soon make their move. As well as stopping the bandits, he had the workers and customers safety to think of. Johnny had a talk with the agent and the employees about the best way to protect themselves. He was hired to do the protecting. They were just to do their jobs and get to cover if shooting started. He told the ones that knew how to use their guns to use them only in self-defense. He did not want an innocent person being hurt because of him.

It was a bright sunny day. Johnny was in the office with only the agent and one clerk. Watching thru the window, Johnny saw the men gathering together across the street. There were five of them and a man down the street on the side of the office. The man down the street was leaning against the hitching rail that had six horses tied to it. He figured four men would come in and one would stay outside the door watching to see if anyone was entering to surprise them.

Johnny had called it right. The clerk went into the storage room and the agent went to the back of the office so he could get down behind a desk. Johnny had his ten - gauge shotgun in his hands; he had a forty-five colt lying on a desk close to where he was standing. His own forty-five and thirty-eight were in their holsters. He was as ready as he could be to stop the bandits. As they came in the office, they pulled their scarves up over their faces. They were surprised that no clerk or agent was at the window. They turned to look around and saw the shotgun pointed at them. The idea that a shotgun at that range could tear up several of them real quick made them pause for a few seconds. Then one pulled his gun up at Johnny, but one barrel of the shotgun went off. The one gunman went down and the one next to him with a loud yell tried to make it to the door. Within seconds the other barrel tore into the other two bandits. The one closest took a direct hit to the stomach. The other man had some of the shot hit him, but not enough to keep him from firing at Johnny. As soon as the shots were fired from the shotgun, Johnny dropped the shotgun and grabbed the forty-five on the desk. The shot from the gunman still caught Johnny in the shoulder, but it was just a nick. Johnny's first shot hit the gunman in the side; the next, in the neck. There was still the one near the door who was bleeding from the shot that was spread over his chest and arms. He threw his gun down and hollered that he needed a doctor. The man, watching the outside, stepped in the doorway, his gun ready to use to help his partners. A shot from Johnny drove him back out the door and tumbling into the street. Johnny knew there was still the one with the horses; but seeing his partner hit the street, he jumped on a horse and was heading out of town. The sheriff was heading to the office to find out what had happened; but it was all over except taking the one to his office and to get a doctor for him. The others needed to be taken to boot hill.

Johnny stood there, blood dripping from the crease in his arm. The thoughts started through his mind again. All those men dead by his hand. He, too, could be dead, never having seen Carrie again. The thoughts of what he was doing and what he turned out to be was troubling his mind. Would it be better to let Donavan go and go back home to Carrie and live a life that they had planned and dreamed of? The answer came to him at that moment.

He was going back home; this violent life was not for him. He asked the agent for a piece of paper and wrote a note to the express boss that he was quitting. His only thoughts were of heading back home, the home that he missed so badly. The main thought was having Carrie in his arms.

The Last of the Hunted

Johnny caught the next stage heading to St. Louis. He would stop and see his friend Jake and the girls and then be heading back to Indiana, his home. A feeling of excitement and nervousness filled his mind and body as the stage was heading east. It would take several weeks of traveling. It would be around Christmas when he got home. It should be a big surprise to Carrie that he was back home.

The unexpected happened at one of the small towns where the stage made a stopover. Going out to get back on the stage, Johnny saw a couple of ladies and a man waiting to board the stage. The man had stepped back to let the ladies board first. As Johnny walked up, the man turned to him, smiled and said "After you, Sir." It was Donavan.

"Donavan" was all that Johnny could say. After months of searching for him and finally giving up on finding him, he stood before him.

Donavan's smile left his face. He knew by the way the name was said that his hunter had found him. As he stumbled backward, his hand went nervously for his gun. Before he could use it, Johnny had two shots in him and that was all that was needed. There were enough witnesses that saw Donavan draw first that there was no problem at it being a fair kill. Johnny told the town sheriff his story of looking for Donavan and about the killings and shootings he had been in. Then Johnny was back on the stage, rolling for home.

Getting to St. Louis took a few days, but finding Jake was easy. Jake was at work in the express office, whistling away, as Johnny entered. A big smile came over Jake's face as he saw his friend.

"Glad you made it back ok. Heard about the different scrapes you were in. And we heard about you finding Taggart and about being back shot. We were worried about you." Jake pausing briefly, then said, "Have you seen my sisters yet?"

"No, just got off the stage. How are the girls?"

"Good as always, both got fellows now. Fraid I'll be living alone one of these days. They're nice fellows though, so I'm happy for them."

"Guess you'll have to be looking for a wife." Johnny said with a smile.

"Not me, too many ladies to pick just one." Jake said laughing.

"Well, I'm heading back to claim just one." Johnny said confidently.

"How long are you in town for?'

"Just long enough to buy a horse and saddle and I'm on my way home." Johnny seemed content with the idea of heading home.

"Sounds good; that's where you belong. You're going to stop and see the girls, aren't you?

"You bet. I'll stop in before I leave."

Johnny walked down the street to the restaurant. The

girls both came over as soon as he walked in. Rylee took his hand as though he had a special place in her heart. Sofia smiled as she saw him and how glad Rylee was to see him.

"What's this I hear about you two young ladies having fellows, huh? Johnny gave both girls a hug, which made Sofia blush.

"We couldn't wait for you forever, and there're two of us and only one of you." After Sofia's statement, Rylee blushed.

"Sofia!" Rylee was taken aback by Sofia's remark.

"Well, I guess you're right. Jake approves of them, so they must be pretty good men."

"They are." Sofia replied.

"How about you girls feeding me and then I'll be on the road to Indiana."

"We'll feed you good, but we want you to bring that bride of yours to St. Louis on your honeymoon. Jake told us about her."

"I can't promise that, but I will try to get her out here one day for a visit. I'll never forget the way you girls and Jake took me in, even though I was a stranger."

"Set yourself down and we'll bring the food, and a glass of milk, right?" Sofia was already on the way to get some food for Johnny.

"Johnny, when will you start back using your real name? You know you'll always be Trace to me." Rylee had tears in her eyes at this farewell.

"As soon as I get into Illinois, then I'm Trace Williams again." Johnny, after eating, said his goodbyes and was on his way back home.

Chapter Nine

The Trip Home

The days of traveling became hard due to a winter storm blowing in from across the plains. The cold and snow slowed Johnny down to the point that whenever he saw some shelter from the storm he would stop and build a fire, so that he and his horse could warm up a little. He had a couple bags of oats he had slung over the back of his saddle. Traveling in weather like this you have to keep your horse protected. Lose your horse and you'll most likely lose your life. The water in his canteen was frozen. He needed a place to stop soon; a place where he could stable his horse and get a room and a good hot meal. The town of Marion should be coming up soon. He needed everything going for him to make it that far as the snow kept getting deeper. How many days the storm would last, he didn't know. To try and wait it out was too much of a chance to take. He knew he had to keep moving on. After resting and warming up, and with his horse fed, he decided to move on. After a few hours, he saw the dim lights of the town in the distance. He would be glad to get off the trail for a while and into shelter.

Entering the town, he headed for the livery stable to

get his horse taken care of. Then he headed for the restaurant. There were very few people in the restaurant because most were home out of the storm. He tried to knock as much snow as he could from his clothes to keep it from melting on the floor of the restaurant.

The owner saw what he was doing and hollered over to him. "Come on in, young man; take your coat off and take the broom and knock the snow off the coat and yourself. Can't keep the floor dry in this kind of weather; hurry and get some hot coffee in you."

"Thank you; sounds great. It seems to be getting worse out there instead of letting up."

"Don't know where you're traveling to, but I think you might consider a little layover. Traveling east or west?"

"East," Trace replied as he took the cup of coffee.

"Going back home?" A voice came from a table where several men were sitting.

Trace looked to see who would know that he was heading home. He saw a man he remembered; it was the preacher.

"How do you do, Sir? I'm surprised that you remember me." Trace walked over to the table and shook the preacher's hand.

"Of course, I'd remember you. You preached me a sermon before you left on your way west. It was a good sermon, and I know a couple living in a nice little house on the edge of town that will be glad to see you. You left quite an impression on them, also."

"Well, I didn't mean to be preachin' at you; I was just concerned about the Whitlocks. I take it they're doing ok."

"Yes, they're fine. I talked to them about your

suggestion and helped arrange the sale of their farm and getting the house they're in. It seems to be working fine."

Good; they are a really nice couple. They're at the stage of life where they need friends close by. I appreciate your helping them."

"You're planning on seeing them before you leave, aren't you? They'd be hurt if you didn't."

"If I can get a room for the night, I'll stop and see them in the morning. Hopefully, the storm will let up and I can start out for home tomorrow. But I do want to stop and see them."

"I think they'd like you to spend the night at their place. They think very highly of you."

"Well, with the weather the way it is, I wouldn't want to track up their house." Trace was a little embarrassed at the suggestion. He felt it would be taking advantage of a friendship.

"Nonsense. I'll take you down in my buggy. I need to get home before I get snowed in here. If I get snowed in, I'd probably have to preach these men a sermon."

"Let him take you, Son; we get his sermon every Sunday. We think that enough for a body." The men at the table were laughing at the comment.

The preacher knocked on the Whitlocks' door and called out, "Sam, Nelly, its Preacher Anderson. I've got a guest for you." The preacher turned smiling at Trace.

Sam opened the door saying, "Well, come on in and get out of that weather."

"I got a young man that needs a roof over his head for the night. Think you can find space for him?" As the preacher spoke, he pulled Trace around and headed him in the door.

Sam Whitlock's face got a glow to it when he saw it

was Trace. "We always have room for that young man; we prayed every day that he'd make it back. Praise the Lord, he's here, safe and sound." Nelly came over and put her arms around Trace even though his coat was wet and covered with snow.

"You two get in here and let me get some hot coffee in you. This is a Christmas gift early for Pa and me. Get those coats off and sit yourselves down and I'll heat up the soup as soon as I get you that coffee. Then Trace can tell us where all he's been." Nelly hugged Trace again; this time he hugged her, too.

"Sister Nelly, I appreciate that offer, but I got to be getting home. I told my wife I wouldn't be long and I know you don't want her getting after me, do you?" The preacher and Nelly were laughing as they joked with each other.

"No, I certainly don't. You tell Sister Loretta that I said hello. And thanks again for our guest, although we think of him as family."

"Goodnight. You let him get some sleep tonight. Don't keep him up all night talking. You hear that, Sam?" The preacher was kidding with Sam, as Sam put his hand on the preacher's shoulder. Walking to the door both of them were laughing. All three were happy that Trace was once again with them. "I'll see you before you leave tomorrow, weather permitting, Trace."

"Trace, you set down so you're near the stove; it will warm you up some. Take off your boots as though you were at home. I'll get that soup I promised you."

"It is really good to see you both again. This house is really nice; you have it fixed up real nice." Trace was glad to see that his friends had a nice home closer to town where they could make friends and have people around in

74

case of a need.

"We were told how you went to Reverend Anderson and asked him to help us. We would've never done it ourselves; we had too much pride for our own good. It has really been nice the last couple of months living here - thanks to you."

"I really didn't do anything to be thanked for. It just made more sense for you to live closer to a town. You'd be good for the town."

"Listen to him; he should have been a politician." Sam laughed and patted Trace on the back.

Trace ate the soup and then had another bowlful. It sure beat eating on the trail. After talking for a while, the subject came up if he found the men he was looking for. Just answering yes seemed to upset Nelly.

"You aren't in trouble, are you?"

"No, each of them had a chance; there were witnesses both times. I'm in no kind of trouble."

"Do ya have to leave tomorrow?" Sam wouldn't have minded it if he didn't leave at all.

Yes, I'm kind of anxious to get home. I haven't heard from Carrie since I left. I'm afraid something's wrong. I don't know what to think." The Whitlocks could see the worry on Trace's face. "I never thought while in St. Louis to pick her up a Christmas gift. Do you think the store in town would have something nice to give her?"

Nelly looked at Sam and he seemed to know what she was thinking. He nodded. Nelly went to a drawer and pulled out a box. Coming over to Trace, she opened the box containing a beautiful gold locket. She took it out proudly and handed it to Trace.

"That's really a beautiful locket; you must be very

proud of that."

"That I am. A very special fellow gave it to me over forty years ago. Of course, I won't say who." That made Sam glow proudly.

"Sam and I want you to take it for Carrie. We have no one to pass it on to now. And we'd be proud if you would take it for her."

"Oh, I couldn't take your locket; I know how much it must mean to you both. It just wouldn't be right." Trace blushed thinking what an honor it is - that they would want to give it to me for Carrie. How proud she would be that they wanted her to have the locket.

"Please, it would honor us if you would. Please." Nelly wanted it to go to Trace and his family. It was like keeping it in her family. Sam nodded for Trace to take the locket. As Trace took the locket, he turned so they wouldn't see the tears swell in his eyes. He turned to them again and hugged Nelly and kissed her on the forehead. He took Sam's hand and held it more than a handshake.

"I doubt if the store would have much in the way of gifts right now. He's still trying to restock after the fire. It's taking him awhile to get restocked. He lost everything. Even the mail got burnt up. It happened right after ya left us. It might have been the very night that ya left in fact." Sam wanted to make Trace feel the need for taking the locket.

Sam knew it was a special time, but he felt it was easier for everyone to say goodnight. "It's getting late. I think we all need to turn in for the night. Nelly will fix ya a good breakfast before ya leave tomorrow, weather permitting and God willing."

Trace went to sleep thinking about the mail burning up; his letter to Carrie was probably in that mail. That could explain, partly, why he hadn't heard from her. But he did mail several other letters to her.

The next morning the dark clouds were gone and the sun was shining. It would still be a rough trip to make due to the deep snow, but Trace wanted to get home as soon as he possibly could. Saying goodbye to the Mr. and Mrs. Whitlock wasn't easy. It was like leaving home. In the few short days that he knew them, he learned to really love them. They were wonderful people and ones that he would always remember. He made a stop at the parsonage to say goodbye to Reverend Anderson, another person that in a few short meetings had become a friend he would have for life. He said his goodbyes and was on the trail leading home.

The miles through the deep snow seemed to go on forever; night came fast at this time of year. It was hard to find a good place to make camp. He finally came to a place that had once been a house, but was now just charred ruins. It had part of a wall still standing that would be a breaker from the winds for him and his horse. He tried to uncover some dry wood to make a fire and cut some limbs from a fir tree to put between him and the ground to make it a little warmer to sleep. He covered his horse the best he could with the saddle blanket. He put his horse in the corner where he had the protection from the wind on two sides. He built his fire between him and his horse, so it would help some from the cold. He was lucky enough to find enough dry wood to last through the night with a good fire. He was hoping that the further east he went, the less snow he would find. He would only know that as he traveled on. He thought as he looked at Carrie's picture "one day closer." The moon shone through the trees leaving its soft light on the snow-covered branches and the surrounding landscape. How could something so beautiful be so cold? He kind of smiled to himself as he shivered and tightened the blankets around him. He fell asleep looking at the tintype that carried Carrie's picture.

Finally Home

Spending several rough days of traveling and he was near Carrie's home. He couldn't wait to see her. It was Christmas Eve. What could be greater than to see her and surprise her for Christmas? The beautiful locket Mrs. Whitlock had given him would be a beautiful gift, even though he didn't buy it for her. It was a great gift. He could see the lights of her house now. He urged his horse a little faster though they were both tired. He felt like getting off and running to the house. The excitement in him kept building. Jumping from his horse and racing up the steps, he knocked on the door.

A man's voice answered the knock on the door with the question, "Who is it?"

"It's Trace, Mr. Johnston."

"Trace who?"

"It's me, Mr. Johnston, Trace Williams."

"The name's not Johnston, its Delaney. What do you want?"

Trace had been away eight months, but he was sure this was the house. "Come on, Mr. Johnston. It's me, Trace. I'm here to see Carrie."

"There's no Carrie here. They moved away about five months ago."

"They couldn't have. I own the farm down the road.

I'm telling you, I'm Trace Williams. Please open the door and talk to me."

The door slowly opened and a man looked him over for a minute, then said to come in. Trace was tired and confused, not knowing what to think.

"I'm sorry to bother you, Sir, but I can't understand why they would sell the farm. They were happy here. I've only been gone a little over eight months. My folks were their best friends, I plan on marrying Carrie."

"You're the boy who left to go after the men who killed your folks, aren't you? I heard talk of you. People were surprised when Johnston up and sold the farms. They moved away leavin' no address with anyone as to where they were going. Folks around here figured you must be dead; being as Johnston sold your farm, too."

"I feel like they might be right. I didn't expect this at all. Would you mind me sleeping in your barn for the night?"

"No, Son, you go right ahead. Let me get you a couple more blankets. Go ahead and feed your horse, too. It had to be rough traveling the last couple of days."

"Thank you, Sir. I'm much obliged."

"Before you go out in the cold again, we'll get you a cup of coffee and something to eat. Let you get warmed up a bit."

"That very nice of you. It's been awhile since I've eaten or had any coffee. Would you mind if I put my horse in the shelter first? He's had it rough, too."

"The barn is off to the left of the house."

"I'm familiar with it; it's where I slept my last night here."

Trace left for the barn thinking how different it is this time. He was still in a bit of shock trying to figure out what had happened. In the morning, he would ride into town and check with the minister and some of his old friends to see if they knew anything about what happened or where he could find Carrie.

The night in the barn bought back memories of Carrie telling him how much she loved him and how she didn't want him to leave. He told her he had to go. She cried, telling him she'd wait for him. If it took forever, she would wait for him. Now eight months later, she was gone. What happened? He had to get the men who killed his mother and dad. Why wouldn't she have waited? Why did Mr. Johnston sell both the farms? The tears came down again as Trace tried to fall asleep. As tired as he was, sleep did not come easy. Words came back to haunt him. The words of the sheriff telling him if he did find and kill the two, his life would be different. Jake's words that if he wore his guns the way he did, he would have to use them. Preacher Anderson telling him "Vengeance is mine, saith the Lord." How did it all happen?

The next morning the sun was shining and would melt some of the snow making the traveling to Salem easier. The ride to town was not a happy one. He had to pass the farm where his mother and father were killed. The place where he thought he and Carrie would be living. Now, he didn't know what to think. What would he do if none of his friends knew where to find Carrie? The first person he would look up was the minister. Surely they would have told the minister where they were moving.

Trace found the minister, but to no avail. Then he looked up Mr. Grayson, the lawyer, only to get the same answer. Mr. Grayson said that he had tried to warn him not to give power of attorney to someone outside the family. But Trace had no family; the Johnstons were his mother and father's best friends. Carrie was to be his family. If he had it to do again, he would do it the same way. The sheriff said he was sorry, but he couldn't help him, because legally Harry Johnston could sell the farm. Trace told the sheriff there was nothing he wanted him to do; he was just trying to find out what happened and where he could find Carrie. After finding no answers to his questions, Trace felt there was nothing for him around Salem anymore.

Trace knew there was one more stop he had to make. It was one that he dreaded. It would be like saying goodbye to his life up to now. With pain even greater than when he got the news of their deaths; Trace knew he had to visit the graves of his mother and father. As he got off his horse and started the walk to the gravesites, his eyes filled with tears. A man who lived the life he's lived the last several months was still brought to his knees at the graves.

Trace started to talk to his folks. His heart was torn apart with hurt and loneliness, but there were words he would want them to hear. "I'm sorry I wasn't here for the service. I felt I had to get them for what they did to you. Well, I got them, but it took a while. I was warned by friends that vengeance could be costly. I don't know what happened to Carrie and her folks. I don't have the farm any more. That doesn't really matter, because you're not there now. It's good that you're both together; I can't imagine your being apart. I'm leaving the area now; there is nothing for me here anymore. I really miss you and always will, but you'll always be in my thoughts and in my heart. Well, so long, I got a long ride ahead of me. Thank you for all the years of love and care." Trace rose slowly with hat in hand and walked away, knowing he might never return.

So, he turned his face westward and figured that was the direction to head. After a disappointing homecoming, he was headed back the way he had just traveled. This time without any purpose or meaning. He didn't have any idea where to start looking for Carrie and her family. He would have to try to find some kind of purpose and meaning to life as he moved on. He was sure that trying to locate Carrie would be a life-long quest. He thought, "I do have some purpose to life after all."

Chapter Ten

The Lonely Trail West

The ride west was not a happy one. Trace kept questioning over in his mind what could have happened. The postmaster in Salem had three letters from him, unclaimed. The first letter must have been burnt in the fire that Mr. Whitlock had told him about. The next letters were mailed from the small towns that he had passed through and could have taken heaven knows how long to get there. Why would they have moved within three months of his leaving? Would he ever run into any of the Johnstons? Where would he even start to look?

Trace felt he might as well winter with the Whitlocks. They were as much family as he had now. They liked him and he certainly liked them. That is where his horse was headed now.

The Whitlocks were surprised to open the door and see Trace standing there – surprised, but happy, to see the young man they thought so much of. After saying how glad they were to see him, they asked "Where's Carrie?" After Trace told his story, they said how bad they felt for him. Trace wanted to give back the locket, but Nelly refused to take it. She said she'd pray that he would find

Carrie somehow and that God had a way of working things out that we can't understand. For now, they were happy that he would be staying with them for a while.

Time seemed to go by slowly for Trace. He tried to fix up things the best he could to help out the Whitlock's. They were as proud as could be to have Trace with them and introduced him to all the neighbors and townspeople. The young ladies were overly eager to meet him, but he just greeted them politely and left it go at that. Sam and Nelly would notice him, at times, just looking at the picture of Carrie for what seemed like hours.

Sam told Trace, "If ya keep cuttin' that firewood, I'll have to start selling it."

Trace said, "Fine, make yourself some money." Sam and Nelly could see Trace was getting restless and knew he would soon be leaving to try to find Carrie or maybe to try and find himself. He certainly looked lost at times.

March finally came around and Trace decided to head on west in search of what, he wasn't sure. He would certainly like to run into Carrie. The west was a big place; it would take a miracle for that to happen. But he bid farewell to his adopted family and headed west for St. Louis and beyond.

St. Louis, this time, was different than his first arrival. He knew he had friends here and was not in search of men he had sworn to kill. He headed to the express office to see his friend Jake. Jake was, of course, talking and joking with all those around. Seeing Trace, he stopped and came over to take his hand. The big smile and the firm and long handshake made Trace feel good to know he was so welcomed.

"I never expected to see you back so soon. Is Carrie

with you?"

"No. I'm afraid that by the time I got back, she was gone."

Jake could see the hurt in Trace' eyes as he answered. He wasn't sure how or what to say next. "I can't leave this early for lunch, and I got some boxes I have to get ready to go out. Go in and say hello to the boss. I'm sure you got a job, if you want one. Then, if you haven't had anything to eat yet, go on down to the restaurant. I'm sure the girls will be glad to see you."

"Yeah, let me say hello to Mr. Gibson and then wash up a little. I am hungry and, of course, I want to see those pretty sisters of yours." With a slap across Jake's back, Trace headed over to the office.

Rylee and Sofia were surprised to see Trace come walking in. They hadn't expected him back this soon.

Rylee exclaimed, "My heavens, never expected to see you this soon. I thought you would be hard at work on that farm and helping to wash dishes." Laughingly, she gave Trace a hug.

Sofia's question was, "Are you and Carrie moving out here, or are you heading further west?"

"Well, I'm here for a few days, then I'm heading farther west. And right now I need a good meal and plenty of it." Trace gave Sofia a big hug. He felt as though they were his sisters as well as Jake's.

"Something happen back home, Trace? Or aren't we to ask?" Rylee knew something was wrong for him to be here by himself.

"Yeah, I went back to nothing. Carrie and her folks were gone and both the farms were sold. So there was no reason for me to stay there anymore. So here I am."

Trace just gave a big sigh and then smiled as though he just accepted it as a fact of life.

"Oh, I'm so sorry; I know how you were looking forward to going home and getting back to your normal life. I am really sorry." She bent over and gave Trace another hug.

There was the chatter of several people entering the restaurant at that moment. Three young men entered, and one came directly over to the table.

Rylee looked up and smiled. "Well, look who's here? What are you doing in so early? I'm glad you are here because I want you to meet a friend of mine. Glenn, this is Trace that you heard us talk so much about. He's passing through again. He just can't stay put." Turning to face Trace, she said proudly, "This is my fellow, Glenn."

Trace stood up and put his hand out to shake hands with Glenn, but only got a cold, hard stare instead. "It's good to meet you. I know you have to be a good man for Rylee to think so highly of you."

"If she thinks so highly of me, why did she have her arms around you?" Glenn's eyes showed the anger of a jealous man.

"Glenn! Trace is a friend of the three of us. A good friend." Rylee was upset at Glenn's reaction to Trace. "Now, you apologize – Now!"

"He'll be the one to apologize, or he can get ready to use that gun he wears strapped down. I won't be made to look like a fool in front of my friends."

"Now, there's no need to talk about using a gun. Jake and the girls have been good friends to me. I feel like they're family. Like she said, 'I'm just passing through'." Trace was not expecting a confrontation like this.

"Glenn, are you crazy? Trace is Johnny Rains; I thought he'd be going back to using his real name. That's why I introduced you to him by the name Trace. I thought he'd be your friend, too." Rylee was truly disturbed to see Glenn's reaction to Trace.

"I don't need any saddle tramp for a friend and no decent girl would be putting her arms around him." It was anger still talking from the young man.

"Now, you listen! And listen good! You can say what you want to about me, but you keep a respectful tongue when you talk about Rylee. Do you understand me?" Trace was riled up over Glenn's comment on Rylee.

"Both of you, stop it! The two people I care so much about talking to each other that way. I didn't appreciate that comment about a decent girl, Glenn. It really hurt." Rylee was almost in tears.

"I'm sorry, I didn't mean to hurt you. I know you're a decent girl; I wouldn't have loved you otherwise. But think how I feel, my friends seeing you with your arms around him. They heard me challenge him. I can't back down now. I have to face him."

"It means enough to die over? He'll kill you. And it's all because of your stupid pride."

"You ever kill anyone, Glenn? Even if you win, it will change you. Believe me, I know. Think it over; I'm tired from a long ride. If you still have a fight in mind, meet me tomorrow where they're planning the new park. Twelve noon. Better say goodbye to Rylee first." Trace turned and walked out of the restaurant.

"You won't be there tomorrow, Glenn; if you love me and still talk of marrying me, you won't be there." Rylee walked back to the kitchen. The customers who had heard some of the talk, because it was rather loud, just looked at Glenn.

Sofia walked passed Glenn and her only comment was, "Fool."

Trace was still hungry since he didn't get to finish his meal; so he checked in at the hotel and then got a sandwich there. By the time he finished his sandwich and had a piece of pie, Jake was there to join him.

"You heard?"

"I told you - my sisters get the word around faster than a newspaper. They said you were heading this way; I take it you're not staying with us."

"With that hot-headed friend of Rylee's, you've got to be kidding?" Trace looked at Jake with a smile on his face

"Well, what are you going to do if he shows at noon tomorrow?"

"At noon tomorrow, I'll probably be ten miles out of St. Louis heading to Colorado. Try my luck in the gold fields." Trace said, having a blank look on his face.

"I'll tell Rylee; she is really upset."

"No, you just tell that pretty girl that I said not to worry; her boy will be fine. Don't tell her I'm leaving. Let them have a chance to work it out. I need to get some sleep. I'll see you in the morning before I pull out." With a handshake they parted. Jake was wishing things were different and Trace could stay.

"See you in the morning, Trace."

"The name is Johnny - - - - - Johnny Rains."

Morning came quickly, and Johnny was sitting on the steps when Jake got to work. "You city boys like to sleep in, don't you?"

"Got to get my beauty sleep; don't want the women to be disappointed." Jake said with a smile. "You ready to head out, huh?"

"Yeah, thought I'd be on my way. You take care of yourself and those sisters of yours. Better get that future brother-in-law of yours not to put so much stock in what his buddies think."

Swinging up into the saddle, Johnny was on his way west. He was riding into an unplanned and unknown future.

The morning in St. Louis was not a quiet scene. Rylee was upset. She had been crying all night. The two men who meant the world to her would be facing each other at twelve o'clock. There could be no good outcome. Jake had told her of the gunfight with the fellow who pushed Trace into a fight. He was dead before he could have figured out what happened. Jake told her of men who tried to rob the stagecoach, of the men Trace was looking for and others. Now, the boy she planned to marry was going up against him. She couldn't persuade either to drop it because of their stupid pride. Sofia tried to comfort her as much as she could, but there wasn't much she could say. She knew Glenn was no match for Johnny Rains. If he had known before talking big to impress his friends, he would never have left it get this far.

Jake came into the restaurant and went and helped himself to a cup of coffee. Seeing Rylee so upset, he put his arm around her and said, "Relax, I'm not supposed to tell you or Glenn, but I can't see my sister this upset and not say anything. Don't worry about the twelve-noon showdown. There isn't going to be any."

Rylee's tear-stained face looked up at Jake, "Why not, what will stop those two?"

"Johnny rode out of town this morning. He would rather people say he backed down from a fight than see you hurt. After all, we're family, aren't we? I think he adopted us the way we adopted him. Let Glenn sweat it awhile."

It was no more than said until Glenn walked into the restaurant. His appearance was of one who hadn't much sleep that night. Rylee ran to him with opened arms, hugged him and said, "If you ever again open your big mouth like that, I'll shoot you myself." Glenn was still unaware that Johnny had left town.

Looking for New Adventure

The ride through Missouri was quiet and uneventful, which was fine with Johnny. He was riding southwest, destination unknown; it was a new year - 1869. What would it have in store for him? The answers laid ahead, not behind. He thought he would take the Santa Fe Trail and try south. Maybe fate would lead him to Carrie and her family.

After days of riding alone, he figured himself to be somewhere in northern Texas. It was a beautiful morning; the air was so fresh, like no one had ever breathed in this great land at all. The land stretched out for miles with nothing in sight except fields of high grass and a few scattered trees. The sound of gunfire broke the silence and his peaceful thoughts. He knew with all of that gunfire it had to mean trouble for someone. Riding to the crest of a hill, he found his answer. In the valley below was a circle of wagons being attacked by thirty to forty Indians. The wagons must have been taken by surprise, as the teams were still hitched to the wagons and a broken and open circle was formed. He figured in this area the

Indians were Comanche. Some of the wagons were already on fire, and without some help, the Indians would surely wipe out the whole train. Riding down the hill to get in range, he stopped, stood up in his stirrups, took aim and fired. He was within distance and one Indian fell from his horse. Each of the next several shots saw targets drop from their horses. Seeing this, three Comanches turned to charge the lone figure that was targeting them. Holding steady, Johnny aimed at the closest one, then another, and then the last one. The Henry proved faithful again. As the riderless horses went by him, he moved in closer. The Comanches, seeing this, stopped and gathered together to see what was to be made of this stranger who showed no fear. They saw him riding toward them, as if to challenge them all. The chief lifted his rifle to him, and turned and rode off, with the others following, leaving the wagon train without further battle. The chief thought that this man must have big medicine with him to ride unafraid into his warriors. Johnny figured he had about nine shots left in his Henry. The Comanche were not used to this many shots from one gun.

Johnny rode in among the wagons to see if he could be of help. The women and older children worked alongside the men trying to put out the fires and save what they could of their possessions. Several of the men had lost their lives and several more had been wounded. The man who seemed to be in charge, a big, whiskered man, nodded to Johnny and said he'd get around to thanking him when he got the wounded taken care of. He was trying to set up some protection in case of another attack. It was amazing and great the way everyone was trying to do their part and helping others that needed it. Johnny helped lift some of the wounded and place them where they would be more comfortable.

They worked for several hours taking care of the injured and getting the wagons ready to travel. The Comanches had driven off their stock and extra horses. They would have to make the teams they had hitched up do until they could get more. So, they would have to travel light and slow. One of the children pointed to the hillside where several braves sat watching what was happening in the wagon train. When they made ready to travel, Johnny rode in the lead, his rifle in his right hand, the barrel resting across his left arm. The Comanches watched, but let them go in peace. As Johnny looked up the hill at the Indians, one raised his rifle above his head, and Johnny did the same. The Indians turned and rode off. That brought a cheer from the people of the train.

Johnny rode along with the wagon train. He was going the same way and the people needed all the help they could get. Johnny rode ahead to keep an eye on things. He spotted an antelope which he was able to bring back providing some fresh meat for the people to share. The wagon master, Jim McGuire, had thanked Johnny many times, along with the many thanks he received from the weary travelers. To the children, he was somewhat of a hero. The young boys followed him around and tried to walk like him and use his expressions. Seeing how little these people had left and yet they were moving on with such great expectations, made him feel proud that he could be traveling among a group like this.

He wondered if somewhere Carrie was experiencing the same kind of problems. He prayed that she was safe, and that someday he would find her. Her picture and her memory were all he had to keep him moving on. At night when they camped, Johnny would take out her picture and sometimes just press it to his heart and think of her. As he stretched out to sleep and heard the sound of a lone wolf howling at the moon, he felt as lonely as the wolf as he tried to drift off to sleep. He knew he would face the dawn of a new day, always searching for his past. He was humming a song that seemed it was written about him.

WITH A SADDLE FOR A PILLOW
AND THE HARD GROUND FOR A BED
THE ONLY LIFE A COWBOY HAS
ARE DREAMS THAT'S IN HIS HEAD
I HEAR A LONE WOLF HOWLING;
HE'S HOWLING AT THE MOON
WE SHARE THE SAME LONELINESS,
WE SHARE THE SAME OLD MOON
YES, I'M JUST A LONELY COWBOY
WITH A DREAM THAT RIDES ALONG
    (DREAM THAT RIDES ALONG

They would soon be at the Metcalf Ranch at Timpas Creek and should be able to get some help and supplies to continue their journey.

Johnny had now acquired the reputation of Indian fighter. This, with the other stories being told of him, added to his legend. The Comanches' stories about Johnny made it seem as if he carried magic powers. Later on in traveling, if his camp was seen by the Comanche and Kiowa, they would ride around and not disturb him.

While in Texas, Johnny rode guard on stage coaches for a while, and then signed on a cattle drive going north to Abilene. He did this knowing that the big drives would soon end. Railroads would be coming to different towns and the cattle could be loaded on closer. It would lessen the chance of losing cattle and men along the way. The railroad connecting the east and the west all the way to California would be finished this year. General Grant was president. Who would have thought he would go from the army to the presidency? Things were really changing in the country - some good, some bad, but in life that's what you get - the good and the bad.

Johnny hoped that this time when he got north, he would run into Carrie somewhere in his travels. As for this job, he wanted to be part of a great cattle drive. He hopes it's worth it. Those who have made it say it's a hard, lonely life. As they headed the cattle north, he figured he would soon find out.

What was said was true. It was being in the saddle from sun up to sun down and then taking your turn riding night watch. It was either hot and dusty or rainy and muddy. There were nice, quiet evenings, too; but it seemed that because of being tired, you noticed the bad times on the trail more. At night, the talk around the fire after supper was friendly. Most of the cowboys were easy-going until they would hit a town and some would get carried away and cause trouble. A few never made it back from town. When it was time to go to sleep, that's when the loneliness would hit. Johnny would take out his picture of Carrie and look at it until he'd fall asleep. For some reason her picture brought to mind his favorite song. It would be going through his mind as he drifted off to sleep.

IN MY SADDLE BY DAY
YOU ARE WITH ME ALL THE WAY
THOUGH THE DAYS ARE LONG AND HARD
IT'S THE WAY I EARN MY PAY
WHILE PUSHIN' THE DOGGIES ALONG
SAD AND LONELY I JUST KEEP A RIDING ON
I'M JUST A LONELY COWBOY
WITH A DREAM THAT RIDES ALONG
(DREAM THAT RIDES ALONG)

The cattle drive finally ended. After getting paid off, several of the boys were trying to figure out what they would do when they got back. Johnny explained that he wasn't going back right now. He liked Texas and may return someday, but for now he was going to stay in the Colorado territory and maybe head north to the Wyoming and Montana territories.

Johnny traveled around to different small towns in the Kansas and Nebraska areas also, always hoping to find Carrie. All his searching was to no avail, his hopes seemed to dim as he traveled on, but he just couldn't give up.

Chapter Eleven

Carrie's Problems Grow

The year 1873 was a promising year for the Johnston's farm in northern Nebraska. If the weather was right, this would be the year that the farm started paying for itself. A good wheat crop would be worth all the hard work Harry had put into the fields. Carrie was on pleasant terms with her dad. He was a good man, who was hurt and disappointed in Trace and her, but showed that he really loved and cared for her. When she gave him a grandson, he was a proud and happy grandfather. As soon as he came in from the fields and washed up, he would spend time with little Harry. Carrie insisted on the name Harry for her father and Thomas for Trace's father. She gave him the last name of Williams. Neighbors accepted the story that her husband was accidentally killed on the way from Ohio to the farm in Nebraska. The people in town showed friendliness to Carrie, especially the young men; but she stayed to herself, still in hopes that someday Trace would show up for her. Except for missing Trace so much, the world she lived in was pleasant and comfortable.

One day Harry came in and told her to take little Harry and go down in the storm cellar. He told her no matter what happened to keep little Harry quiet and don't come out of the cellar, no matter what she heard.

She asked him, "What's the problem?"

He said, "There's no time to explain; just get down there and be quiet."

After closing the door on the cellar, Harry laid a rug over it. Sara had been out back and had just come in. Harry told her, "Hurry down to the storm cellar; some Indians are heading our way." He went to move the rug and saw one Indian looking in the window. It was too late to hide Sara.

Sara remarked, "I thought the Indians had been moved out of Nebraska."

Harry replied, "It's probably some that drifted down from the Dakotas. Carrie and little Harry are in the cellar. I'll go out and talk to them, and maybe if I give them some food and tobacco, they'll ride off."

As soon as Harry opened the door, he was shot by one of the Indians. It was not so quick for Sara. Carrie, hearing the screams, covered little Harry so he wouldn't hear the screaming and tried to keep him quiet. She knew there was no way to help her mother and dad.

She hid in the cellar for what seemed like hours, and then finally heard the voices of white men. She heard one man say that there must have been a child here because there was a small bed in the one room and some toys. She called out from the cellar and finally the door was lifted up for her and little Harry to come up. A man in his midthirties was the first one she saw. He took little Harry and handed him to another man and then helped Carrie up the steps. As she came out of the cellar, she saw the covered bodies on the floor. The man told her not to look at the bodies, but to go outside. He asked one of the men, who was a neighbor that she had seen talking to her father one day, to take her and the baby back to his house where the women could help them. They would come back and bury the couple after they caught up with the Indians. The Indians were on a murder raid and hit another farmhouse killing everyone there. How many more places, they didn't know. The men wanted to catch up with the Indians before they got back to the Dakotas, so, they left right away.

The one man stayed for a couple minutes and introduced himself as James Barton. His family lived twenty-some miles west of the Johnston farm. He said that he'd look in on her when he got back. Carrie was still scared and in shock at losing her parents. First, Trace's parents, then Trace gone, and now her parents, what was she to do now? How would she and little Harry survive? She couldn't run the farm. Even with hired help, she couldn't live on her own and take care of little Harry. Where was Trace? How could he have left her? She was in a daze and was not even crying over the loss of her parents.

She said nothing as a man got the wagon ready to take her to his farm. He asked what she would need to take with her, and she just looked at him, unable to think what she would need. He didn't ask again; he just helped her in the wagon and then lifted little Harry into the wagon. As the wagon pulled away from the house, she thought, another home I'm leaving. This time alone, except for little Harry. How would she survive without her parents?

The man and his family took Carrie and Harry in and

tried to make them comfortable. They fed them and made a place for them to get some sleep. Little Harry fell asleep quickly, but sleep did not come to Carrie. She laid down, but her mind was still hazy; the screams of her mother kept echoing in her ears. Then, after laying there for hours, she heard some horses approaching the house. Was it more Indians? She jumped up and grabbed little Harry and hid in the corner. The man who had brought her to the house heard her making a noise as she had jumped up. He came into the room and told her everything was all right. It was just the neighbors returning. They had caught up with the Indians who were drunk from the whiskey that they must have stolen from one of the houses. They wouldn't be doing any more killing. James Barton came in to ask how she was doing and if she had any family nearby. She finally answered that she had no family anywhere. He asked about her boy's father and his family. She just answered, no family. James asked if she would like to come and stay with his family until she decided what she wanted to do and what she would do with the farm. He seemed kind and concerned about her, so she shook her head yes.

Carrie and little Harry arrived at the Barton home and were welcomed by James' mother and father. Also, at the home were his three brothers and two sisters. They all tried to help Carrie and Harry adjust to the new surroundings. James was the oldest of the family and carried a lot of the responsibility of the farm. They had been quite successful since moving to Nebraska. James was not a big man but had both physical strength and strong character. James was soft spoken and mild mannered. His sisters kind of smiled when they would see him with Carrie, which would make him blush and usually leave the room.

Carrie was still having problems dealing with the loss of her mother and dad. She realized that if she had not brought the shame of an unwed pregnancy to the house, they would have still been in Indiana and her parents would be alive. As the months passed, Carrie was more at ease with the family and tried to do her share of chores. James finally told her he needed to talk to her about her parents' farm. What would she like to do with it? She had no idea what to do with the farm or where she would go. She knew her father had some money in the bank and the sale of the farm would bring her some money. But where would she live and how long would the money last? She knew her mother had some sisters that lived in Rhode Island, but she had never met them and felt no ties that would have wanted her to try and go to them as family. Her dad's brother was in Rhode Island also, but she felt the same about him. Going there would be going to a strange place and strangers.

James took Carrie's hand and said to her in a soft caring way, "Carrie, out here in the west it is different than back east or even Ohio. It is a rough land yet and decisions have to be made many times of necessity. I cared very deeply for you the moment I saw you. If you would agree to it, I'd marry you and become a father to little Harry. I've some money saved and we could buy a piece of land of our own or live here for a while with the family." Carrie knew James was sincere in his offer and that he would make a fine husband and father. Carrie knew she could never marry anyone without being completely honest with them. But how could she explain why they were in Nebraska and about Harry and his father.

"James, I really appreciate your offer, and I believe you are a fine man. There are so many things I would have to explain, and then you might not want to keep the offer open." The hurt look in Carrie's eyes told James that there was more to Carrie's story then she had told.

"I can't believe that anything you could tell me could make me change my mind about the two of you. If you want to tell me, fine; if not, think about my offer and what else you would consider doing. If it is yes, it would make me very happy; if no, I will try to help you in any way I can." Taking hold of her shoulders and bringing her close to him, he kissed her gently on the forehead and said, "You think on it; I won't rush you."

"James, we were not from Ohio. I have never been to Ohio; I'm from a farm near Salem, Indiana. We had a farm there and down the road from our farm was the Williams' farm. The couple who owned the farm were best friends with my folks. They had a son the same age as me. I loved him as long as I can remember. He was always big for his age and he always looked out for me. I can remember one time, we were about ten or twelve years old, a drummer came by with his wagon of goods. Of course, I wanted to see what all he had. Trace didn't like the way he looked or talked to me. I didn't think anything was wrong and went to the back of the wagon with him to see what all he had. He put his arms around me and started hugging me. Trace followed and had a pitch fork. He put the pitch fork against the man ribs and told him to back off and get on his wagon or he would put the pitch fork through him. The man did as Trace said. And it was always, just Trace and me. One day, when we were seventeen, two men killed his parents. Trace felt that he had to avenge his parent's deaths. There was no talking him out of it. He stayed the night in my parents' barn before leaving. I went out to be with him before he left. He left the next morning; I never heard from him again. Soon, I found out I was carrying Harry. My father was so ashamed of me that he sold the farm. In fact, Trace's farm, too, and we moved without letting anyone know where we were going. I never heard from Trace again. My father thought it was better to tell people my husband died on the way. I could never marry you without your knowing the kind of person I am. I'm the cause of my parents' deaths. And I still love Trace and always will."

"I understand and know what kind of person you are. You are a wonderful, honest and loving person. I believe Trace is probably dead, or he would have come back for you. You are not to blame for your parents' deaths. You said that Trace's parents were killed in Indiana, were you responsible for that? Tragedy can happen anywhere, any time. We have to live life the way it comes to us, as it comes to us. I would be proud for you to be my wife." This time James took Carrie in his arms and kissed her and said how much he really loved her.

Carrie agreed to marry James. After talking over the plans for their future, they agreed to move to Texas and buy a ranch and give James his dream of having his own ranch. It would be a new start for the three of them, James, Carrie and Harry Barton.

Chapter Twelve

The Move to Texas

The year 1875 was the beginning of the new life for the Bartons. They were on their way to Texas to the new ranch that James had bought. James made a quick trip down to Texas with two of the men that worked at Barton's farm in Nebraska. The two men, brothers, were from Texas and came north for work after the Civil War. Times were rough for the people of Texas at that time. The northerners were taking advantage of the conditions and profiting from the misfortune of the people. Ed and Bill Marshall rode with General John Bell Hood and served the Confederacy proudly. They lost their younger brother, Jim, at the Battle of Chickamauga. Returning home at the end of the war, they found it hard to find work. The small ranch the family had before the war was gone. So were both their parents due to a flu epidemic that had hit the area. With nothing left and no job prospects, they headed north ending up in Nebraska working for the Bartons. The Bartons were fair people and did not carry the war over into the peacetime as many did. James had many conversations with the Marshalls about Texas and cattle ranching. When Carrie had agreed to marry him, James decided to fulfill his dream of having a cattle ranch. So, with Ed and Bill, he made the trip to Texas and bought the ranch. Now back, he bought a wagon to move his family and the two hired hands to Texas. Both Ed and Bill were already close to Carrie and young Harry. After the work was done and the brothers were relaxing, Harry spent many hours with them. Each of the men felt like he was an uncle to Harry instead of a hired worker. Bill commented to Ed one time, "You know she's not our sister," to which Ed replied, "You have to admit, she sure reminds you of Callie." Callie was their sister who now lived in California and had a girl and boy of her own. Though they didn't say it, they both loved Carrie as a little sister. Her soft, gentle-caring ways made her easy to love.

The trip to Texas held the possibility of many dangers. They traveled west and then south to avoid the nations. The Texas panhandle could be just about as bad. Then down through Texas was the fear of the Comanche. Though the trip was long, it was made without any bad trouble. A broken wheel and some bad storms and they were finally at the ranch. It was a little outside the town of Pecos. For the most part, people were friendly. The Marshalls knew some of the people and made it easier for the Bartons to get adjusted to the area and the people. The ranch was a small one. The former owner had just recently lost his wife and no longer desired to stay on. The house had a kitchen, sitting room, and two bedrooms. There was a bunk house big enough to house ten hands. It was decided that since the Marshalls were the only hands, at present, Carrie would cook and the five of them would eat at the house. Ed and Bill were more like family than hired hands anyway. Hopefully more hands could be added, but for now they would have to be enough.

The ranch was growing with more cattle each year. A couple more hands were added. Carrie was still the main cook and Ed and Bill continued to have their meals in the house. They also continued being uncles to young Harry, who was growing fast, and wanting to learn to ride, shoot and be a regular cowboy.

At times, Carrie would look at Harry and see so much of Trace in him. His hair, eyes and build were that of his father. At a young age, it was easy to tell he would be built much bigger than James. Now, Carrie was carrying James' child. He was as excited as an expectant father could be. He loved Harry and treated him as his own, but was excited at the fact that he was the actual father of the new baby.

The winter of '78 was a sad one for the Bartons and their hands. The baby, born in the fall, caught the fever in December and was gone before the New Year. It was definitely a bad time for all. With a baby comes a lot of hopes and dreams; the loss of one brings much heartache.

The 80s brought a new problem for the Barton ranch and the other ranches in the area. A new man in town started to buy up some ranches around the area. There was talk that force was being used to get the ranchers to sell. The man, a Mr. Colby, had come to the area with money and two men working for him. Jess and Jim, the Walker brothers, were gunmen. They let it be known by the way they wore their guns and the talk they made. Jess had several gunfights, mainly with cowboys that he goaded into the fights. Killing them seemed to have no effect upon him, his brother or his boss. Some believed the killings were just to put fear in the ranchers that Colby was dealing with. James Barton was one of the ranchers who had received an offer for his land from Colby. James Barton had no intention of selling his ranch. Then things seemed to start happening. James added on a couple more hands, but still cattle were missing, fences cut and his hands harassed while in town. Things seemed to be building for a showdown. The problem was that James and his men weren't good gunhands. Things would soon come to a head as the pressure from Colby increased.

Chapter Thirteen

Time Marches On

The years 1870, '71, and '72 came and went quickly. Johnny was the sheriff in several small towns and worked as a security guard on the railroad. In the spring of '71 Johnny became the town marshal in Leadville. That made Stella very happy. After not seeing him except for a short visit in late 1869, she was happy that he would be staying put for a while. Johnny tried to keep their relationship on a friendship basis, but it was plain to see Stella would like it to be more.

On Christmas Eve, the church was having its special service. They had a new minister, a young man who had recently entered the ministry, and this was his first church. He was a friendly young man, whom Johnny had gotten to know quite well. He had asked Johnny to be there for the service. Being invited to the service, Johnny thought that Stella might also enjoy going. Stella was nervous about going; the townspeople did not look on her approvingly. Working at a saloon gave a certain impression to people. Johnny said that she should go and enjoy the service and, maybe, make some new friends. Excited that Johnny would take her someplace like church, she bought a new dress. It was one that a rancher's daughter would wear. She also decided on a new hat. She hoped Johnny would approve, and he did.

At the church, some people gave Stella a look of surprise that this saloon girl would come to their church. The minister, Scott Stewart, read the Christmas story from the book of Luke. Then, as he spoke, he reminded people that Jesus came to save the world - not just a certain class of people, but all people. Anyone that came to Him was welcomed, regardless of their past. In this season of love, it should be in His people's hearts to get those who weren't church members to want to find this love that Jesus had brought to earth. Johnny knew the minister was saying to welcome this girl from the saloon and show her love and acceptance. Even though Johnny was hired to keep the peace in the town and protect the people, they didn't fully accept him as one of their upstanding citizens. The message did get through to many of the congregation, and at the end of the service, they were greeted by many and asked to return. The minister greeted them and thanked Johnny for bringing Stella with him. He said he would like to see them come on a regular basis.

Stella looked a little embarrassed and said, "I enjoyed it and I haven't gone to church much since my mother died.

Scott looked at her and smiled saying, "I hear you have a beautiful voice. Maybe you could sing for us some Sunday."

"Well, I don't know; what would your people say?"

"Probably, that they loved it and want to hear more" Scott gently took her hand. "I'm looking forward to getting you a practice time with some of our songs. You may remember some of them. Stop by the church, if you can, maybe tomorrow, and we'll talk about when we can get together." Stella found herself blushing as Scott held on to her hand.

As they walked away, Stella looked at Johnny and commented, "He didn't treat me like a saloon girl. He was like you, Johnny; he had a softness and warmth about him."

"Yeah, I kinda noticed that, too. He didn't hurt your hand hanging on to it like that, did he?" Johnny smiled making Stella blush even more.

"Johnny, you know that since I met you, you're the only man I wanted to spend my life with. I know you told me that you just couldn't make any kind of commitment until you knew what happened to Carrie. I really believe that all we'll ever be is friends. I'm grateful to have such a great friend and hope that I'll always have you for a friend."

"You will, and I couldn't have a better friend."

As the weeks went on, Johnny often saw the minister and Stella meeting to have lunch. Wanting to leave the saloon, she asked Johnny if he could see about getting her the job of doing the books for the express office and some hours at the general store. Johnny checked right away and used his influence to get her the jobs.

Johnny felt a restlessness that made him want to move on. He resigned as town marshal and said goodbye to his friends and was on the trail again.

A trip back to Marion in '72 to see his friends, the Whitlocks, was a sad visit. Sam had passed on after suffering a heart attack. Nelly had moved into the boarding house. It was good for her; she wasn't alone. She earned her keep by cooking and helping take care of the rooms. Of course, being Nelly, they all loved her there and appreciated having her around. He had also stopped in St. Louis. Rylee had married Glenn, and Glenn showed no anger or jealousy towards Johnny. Sofia was soon to be married. Both the girls had found nice young men that would be good husbands and fathers. Jake was still fancy-free, but it didn't seem that it would be for long. The daughter of the new express agent for the railroad had her sights on him, and he didn't seem to mind it one bit.

In the spring of 1874 a letter caught up with Johnny. It was from Stella, an invitation to her wedding. Scott was asked to take a bigger church in Ogallala, Nebraska. He wanted Stella to go there as his bride. She had, at first, thought of having Johnny give her away, but Mac had just assumed it would be him. He had become like a father to her after her dad had died, so she couldn't hurt him. Anyway, Scott wanted Johnny to be his best man. Johnny was happy for them and would in no way refuse their request.

The West was changing fast; there were new towns with many new people. Railroads were crisscrossing the land making travel easier. It made jobs hard to find for his old friend, Stan Hollister, who had driven coach for quite a few years. Now, he was driving freight wagons wherever he could get a job that the railroad didn't cover. The James boys were still at their trade. In 1873 they robbed their first train. It seemed they were making a habit of it. They were mainly to the east of where Johnny had been roaming, so he never ran into them. The Indians in the Missouri, Kansas and Nebraska areas were mainly driven out and soon would be cut down to almost nothing in Colorado. The Dakotas were still having their problems as the Sioux and the Northern Cheyenne were still fighting to keep their homelands. Changes were coming so quickly, a person could see why the Indians, who have roamed the land freely for so many years, could not adjust to it. With right and wrong on both sides, it ended in a lot of bloodshed. Even between the white men, there has been a lot of blood spilt. Johnny never thought that so much would have been at his hands. Someone had to stop the people who preyed upon the innocent people that could not protect themselves against this element. He had always tried to avoid killing, if he could, but it was the way of life for many. In all the towns he traveled to, he still held hopes that he would find Carrie. He still carried her picture and his memories of her.

His travels eventually took him to the Dakotas and back to guarding express wagons. The gold strikes had created towns and jobs, but also the need to protect the gold shipments from the bands of outlaws who wanted the gold without having to dig for it. The gold in the Dakotas also caused fighting between the white man and Indians. The Indians were trying to protect the little land they had left and their way of life, and actually their lives.

In 1876, Johnny met a man who was quite prominent, George Armstrong Custer. He was a cocky sort of man, not one to Johnny's liking, but he took an interest in Johnny. He told Johnny that he had heard he was an Indian fighter and asked if Johnny was interested in going along with him on what might be the last big battle with the Indians. He was going north to battle with the Sioux and Northern Cheyenne. He told Johnny that it might add to his already big reputation. Johnny refused the invitation and said he was heading back south again. He had no interest in chasing down Indians to kill. Custer dismissed his comment in a casual sort of way.

A while later Johnny heard the news: the last big battle Custer spoke of, did not go well for Custer. Sitting Bull and Crazy Horse had their own ideas for the battle. Custer and all his men were wiped out. The victory for the Sioux would be short-lived. The military of the United States was just too much for the Indians to fight against. Yet, it seemed they had nothing to lose by fighting; they were losing everything they had anyway. Yes, the times were changing, and yet to him at times, it seemed that everything stayed the same.

That year also saw the James – Younger gang get shot up in an attempt to rob a bank in Northfield, Minnesota. People were getting together to stop the outlaw element that the Civil War had bred. There was still a need for law and order in some of the out-lying areas of the West and that's where Johnny mainly found his livelihood.

The 1880's kept changes coming fast; the invention of the light bulb seemed to trigger many other inventions. The big news in 1882 was the assassination of Jesse James. He had needed to be stopped for years, but what upset a lot of people was that he was shot in the back by a friend. No matter how people tried to glorify him, he was an outlaw and in no way a hero. A new outlaw was making a name for himself in the southwest, a young man they called 'Billy the Kid.' The life he chose would surely send him to an early grave.

Johnny's travels had taken him to the Arizona

territory. Frontier territory seemed to hold an attraction for Johnny. His travels from town to town still left him with no signs of Carrie. Hope seemed to fade as the years passed by. Yet the years could not erase the memory of her. As the years passed by, he was working his way north through Texas. Tired of the saddle and the camping out at night, he decided to stop in a town. A good hot bath, a good meal and a good bed for a good night's sleep sure sounded good the more he thought about it. The town of Pecos was just a short distance ahead and a peaceful evening would be nice.

Chapter Fourteen

The Unexpected Happens

The Four Aces Saloon was booming; the Walker brothers were throwing another party. Every time another small rancher sold out, they had money to spend. The Walker brothers were the toughest men in Pecos, Texas, and they worked for Theodore Thomas Colby. Colby, the owner of the Four Aces Saloon, was the richest man around and he wanted to be richer. Being Colby's men, the Walker brothers pressured the ranchers and anybody else Colby wanted out, and then Colby bought the land. Several tried to hold out, but couldn't because of ranches burnt, accidents happening, and some even being foolish enough to be forced into a showdown with the Walker brothers. The last one to face the Walker brothers was a rancher by the name of Barton. Barton was a good man, but he was no hand with a gun. Jess Walker had off two shots in Barton before he could clear leather.

Tonight was a happy time at the Four Aces Saloon, but at the Barton ranch, it was a sad time. That afternoon James Barton was buried. Colby came by the ranch that same afternoon and made his offer to buy them out. Barton's wife, Carrie, told him to leave their land; under no condition would she sell to him. Colby looked over at her seventeen-year-old son and commented that it could be a dangerous place for a growing boy. Harry, Carrie's son, started after Colby. But Carrie stepped in front of him, pressing on him to keep him back. Harry was big for his age and he didn't look much like his father, James Barton. He had dark hair and grayish blue eyes that showed strength uncommon in someone so young. His wild streak was held in check by his mother and father. Even Carrie knew it wasn't over according to Colby, and it wasn't over according to Harry Barton.

The Barton ranch was small. Barton had run the ranch using only six hands. Two of the hands, Bill and Ed Marshall, were like part of the family. They had their meals in the house most of the time with the Bartons. They didn't have any idea how to hold the ranch together now that Barton was dead. They tried to be a strength and comfort to Carrie and Harry, but they were afraid Harry would be hard to control. He would want to take vengeance for his father's death. They couldn't blame him for that, but the chance of his doing it was slim. His friends would be pushing him to challenge the Walker brothers. Bill had taught Harry the best he could on how to use a gun, but even the teacher was no match for either of the Walker brothers. Harry was fast, but lacked the experience to take on the two. Yet, they were afraid he would try. After dinner, he said he was going into town for a while. Carrie tried to stop him, knowing the Walker brothers would be trying to start a fight with him any way they could. His friends would be telling him to take them on. After Harry left, Carrie asked Ed to hitch up the buggy so she could go to town.

Johnny Rains had just arrived in town and was going to have a drink and see about a room. He was tired and thirsty after the long ride. He'd be glad to get a room and bath and get some sleep. He was thinking what his plans should be as he got down from his horse and started to tie it up to the hitching post.

Then he spotted her. There was no doubt about it; it was Carrie. Eighteen years of searching and hoping and it finally happened. She was right there before his eyes. He just froze in the position he was in, staring, wondering if he should approach her. What would he say after all these years? Was she married? How did she end up in Texas? What was she doing going into a saloon? This he had to find out.

Tying his horse to the hitching post, he walked into the Four Aces saloon. Going to the bar and ordering a beer, he watched what was going on. There he saw a young man standing talking to two older men. All three were wearing guns tied down. The crowd stepped aside to get out of the line of fire. They knew that any minute lead would be flying.

"Jess, I'm calling you out for murdering my father." Harry had called the play.

"Well, I killed one Barton this week, I guess I can make it two." Jess just laughed, looking at his brother and Colby.

"You'll have to, Jess, or die trying. You'll find that this Barton is different. I'm not soft and kind like my father was." Harry stood firm and determined, his forty-five colt hung low on his hip, his hand ready to move at any second.

"Carrie ran to the side of the young man and stood in front of him, hugging him and crying, "Please, Harry, don't get yourself killed. I couldn't stand it - losing your father then you." She clung to him, begging him not to face the gunmen.

"Get her back, fellows." Harry then looked at Carrie. "Mother, I made a challenge; I can't back down now."

"Yeah, Mother, let's see if your little boy is a man or not." Jim Walker wasn't as mean or tough as Jess, but he was bad enough. Both were poised waiting for Harry to make his move.

Harry's friends took Carrie and pulled her away from him, so he could continue the fight. Just as Harry went to say to Jess to make his play, a gun butt hit the back of his head sending him to the floor. Everyone was surprised that the stranger had interrupted the fight.

Johnny looked at the two young friends. Whirling his colt and dropping it quickly into his holster, he said, "Get him up and put him in the buggy to go home. Now!" The two did not question it for a minute when they saw the man who said it.

Carrie fell to the floor, crying over seeing her son hurt. "His head; it's bleeding." Looking up at the stranger who had hit him, her crying stopped, and she just stared into the eyes she had not seen in eighteen years.

"It's better his head bleeds a little than to have a belly full of lead." Johnny saw what he had dreamed about all these years, but this was not like he had ever dreamed it to be.

Ed came in and saw Harry being carried out and he feared the worst. He came and helped Carrie off the floor and said that he hadn't heard any shots. Carrie was still just staring at the stranger in disbelief. After all these years, he was just standing in front of her. As tall and handsome as ever, only his face showed that he spent many days out on the trail and that had hardened it.

"Miss Carrie, are you alright? You shouldn't be in a place like this, I should never have left you come in here. Especially alone." Ed was concerned as he felt responsible for her now.

"I'm ok, Ed, really I'm ok." Carrie's tears had now turned into a soft smile. "And thank you, Sir, for stopping the fight. You probably saved my son's life." Carrie turned again to see the stranger in town as Ed was taking her out of the Four Aces.

Colby and the Walker brothers were still taken by surprise at the action of the stranger. When a gun fight is about to take place, no one usually walks into the middle of it.

Jess finally spoke up and broke the silence that had fallen over the saloon as everyone was just watching to see what would happen now. "You know I really don't like having someone stick his nose into my business."

"There are a lot of things in life we don't like, but we either learn to live with them or die with them. It's a choice we have to make." Johnny stood looking at the two standing facing him, the same ones that had been facing the young boy.

Colby quietly said, "You two set down." He was disappointed that it had ended there because Carrie Barton would certainly have sold out after that. But this tall stranger, dressed in black and covered with trail dust, ended that. This stranger may, for a price, be a help to him. The strange gunman turned easily and went back to the bar.

A Mexican, who had done some work for Colby, came up to the table. "Pardon, Senor Colby, Senor Jess, be careful of the man in black. I have seen him before.

He came into Sonora looking for three men; he was wearing a badge then. They came out on the street to meet him and he killed them all, and then hung them over their horses. He went into a cantina, got something eat, and rode out of town as though nothing had happened. The Federales just watch, they didn't say anything about him not being the law in Mexico. He is the one that the Comanche fear, his name is Johnny Rains.

"So, that's the great Johnny Rains. He doesn't look so tough to me." Jim Walker looked at Colby and smiled.

"There are dead men in about ten states that thought the same thing. They say he is a real gentleman, yet the ladies avoid him because they feel it would bring shame on them to know him. Men avoid him because they're afraid of making a mistake and offending him." Colby knew the reputation that followed Johnny Rains. "Ask him to come over and have a drink with us. Maybe he needs a job. His name associated with ours might put the fear of God into these last few holdouts."

The Mexican slowly walked over to the bar and excused himself, not wanting to offend Johnny in any way. "Senor, pardon, Mr. Colby over at that table would like to buy you a drink and talk to you, por favor." After saying what he had to say, he dropped his head and slowly backed away. Then, he went quickly to a table where his friends were sitting.

Johnny looked at the table and then slowly walked over to where the three were sitting. "You wanted to talk to me?"

"Yes, have a seat and let me buy you a drink." Colby gave Johnny a friendly smile, but received none in return.

"I'm ok standing and I just had a drink."

"Well, have another, I want to talk to you, maybe

offer you a job."

"Too big a job for these two boys to handle?"

Jess kicked back his chair, and stood. His face was red with anger, "There's no job too big for me to handle."

"Jess, sit down, we are just talking to the gentleman, not looking for a fight."

"What's the job?" Johnny thought it would give him an idea of what was going on.

"I'm having some problems with some of my neighbors, and I thought a name like yours might carry some weight with them. You, with me, it might even save a few lives. For right now, all you would have to do is ride with me when I go to talk to these people. Of course, if there's a problem, I would expect you to handle it. The pay would be good, I assure you."

"Are you talking to families like the, what was the name, Barton?" Johnny thought he caught the name right.

"Yes, them for one; there are others. I plan on buying their land and some are being stubborn."

"Well, them for one, if they don't want to sell, they won't have to. I'll guarantee that." Johnny spoke in a calm, steady voice and Colby had no problem getting his meaning.

"Well, we'll have to see about that, won't we? Colby tried to match the calmness of Johnny's statement. He just smiled as Johnny backed away from the table.

As Johnny left the table, Colby looked at Jess and said, "I guess I'll have to send a telegram in the morning."

Ed borrowed a wagon and team from one of the Barton's neighbors to take Harry home instead of trying to take him in the buggy. Carrie rode in the wagon pressing on the cut on Harry's head and putting some cold water on it to try to bring him around. She was upset over Harry being hit on the head and she wondered where Trace appeared from. Ed spoke to Carrie and asked her why she thought the stranger stopped the fight. Him being a gunman, he probably works for Colby. Carrie replied, "He's no gunman."

Ed answered, "I heard someone say as we were leaving the saloon that he was Johnny Rains."

"It couldn't be, it just couldn't be." Now, Carrie was more confused than ever.

By the time they got back to the ranch, Harry had regained consciousness. His head was still throbbing from the hit on the head. He asked what happened. "I was standing facing the Walker brothers, Jess mainly, and now I'm with you in back of someone's wagon."

"Ed borrowed the wagon from the Harpers. You wouldn't have fit real well in the buggy, since you were in no shape to sit up. Here, let me help you sit up a little." Carrie was trying to make him as comfortable as possible.

"What happened to my head? I don't remember anything." Harry was still trying to find the answers to his questions.

"You were hit on the head to keep you from getting killed."

"Who did it? Why would someone hit me on the head to stop the fight? It must have been one of Colby's men."

"No, he isn't one of Colby's men. Just forget about him for tonight. You need to get in the house and rest. We'll talk tomorrow." Carrie wondered what she would tell Harry. What would Trace do? Have the years made a difference to him? Is he married? Where does he live?

She had a lot of questions, but none that could be answered until Trace and she met again. Now she wondered when that would be.

Trace had no intention of losing track of Carrie again. He inquired as to the location of the Barton ranch. In the morning, he planned on riding out to find out what had happened then and what was happening now. It looked like Carrie needed some help. This kind of help he was used to providing.

Chapter Fifteen

Johnny's Surprise

The following morning saw Colby going to the telegraph office, and Johnny Rains riding out of town in the direction of the Barton ranch.

At the Barton ranch, the morning was quiet, each waiting for someone to say something. Trying to make conversation without really talking, Carrie commented on what a beautiful morning it was. Harry still had a sore head and was still upset. He knew that Colby would still be trying to pressure them into selling. And he was still wondering who hit him in back of the head. Ed was still trying to figure out if it was really Johnny Rains and where Mrs. Barton knew him from. The stranger sure showed nerve whoever he was.

As they sat eating, Harry could wait no longer, "Ok. Who was the person that stopped the gunfight and why?"

Carrie replied, "I believe we will have a visitor this morning, and we will try to sort things out then."

Bill said, "Well, if it is Johnny Rains, whose side is he on? It's bad enough dealing with the Walkers, but Rains? You know that Ed and I will try to do all we can to save the ranch, but we aren't gunmen. And, Harry, you are out of pace with the Walkers, let alone if Rains gets mixed up in it."

"I don't believe it was Johnny Rains. I believe it is a friend of mine from a long time ago, and he wouldn't be siding with Colby against us." Carrie was sure that no matter what he now called himself, Trace would never be against her.

As Ed looked through the screened door, he saw a rider in black riding up the road to the ranch house. "I think we'll soon have an answer to our questions, one way or the other."

Johnny rode up to the hitching post and tied his horse. Taking his hat, he tried to knock the loose trail dust from his clothes and then smoothed back his hair. He looked more like a young man come a courtin' than a feared gunslinger. Even with his long stride, he took slow deliberate steps coming to and up the porch steps.

Carrie, seeing him coming, was waiting at the door to let him in. She knew by the walk that she was not wrong. Her heart was beating as though it was a young man coming to take her to a social. Though all her problems were still there, she felt a feeling of excitement and that all would be right in the world.

As Johnny went to knock on the door, it was opening and he saw a face that took him back years. It still had the same beauty he remembered, though it showed some years of maturing.

"Please, come in." Smiling, she asked, "Have you had breakfast yet?"

"Oh, just some coffee would do, thanks."

"What are you doing, Mother? You invite a gunfighter to sit down at your table as though he were a neighbor."

"Harry, he's no gunfighter; he's an old friend and I expect you to treat him as such. Would you please tell these people your name?" Carrie wanted to get all the confusion settled now.

"The name's Johnny Rains." Then looking at Harry, after hearing his comment, said, "You talk of gunfighters at your table, what were you trying to be last night? Your friends talking you up as a fast man would have gotten you killed last night. The only reason I stepped in was that I knew your mother didn't want that to happen."

"I can take care of myself without anyone interfering. My friends have seen me draw. I'm fast and I can show you how fast." Harry had put out another challenge. He stood up to get his gun.

Carrie grabbed him and told him to set down. Fear filled her eyes as she said, "I want both of you to promise me right now, that no matter what happens, you won't fight one another. I want that promise from both of you - right now, please, right now."

Both men came to take her in their arms and calm her down. This Harry couldn't understand. Harry just said "ok", and Johnny said "Anything you want."

Carrie asked that everyone leave so she could talk to Mr. Raines. She knew that no matter what he called himself now, he was Trace Williams, the boy she always loved and always would.

Once alone, Carrie took Trace in her arms, "No matter what you call yourself or why you are Johnny Rains, you will always be Trace to me. Holding you and letting you hold me makes me feel like a shameless hussy after just losing my husband; but I can't help it. I wanted to go to your arms last night in that dirty saloon. I wanted to ask you why you never came back for me. Whatever happened, no letters, nothing? How could you have forgotten me? I loved you so much."

"I've never forgotten you. I sent letters and I did go back. Back to nothing. You had gone; the farms were sold. No one knew why or where your family moved. I never went into a town without the thought that maybe you'd be there. I spent my life alone, always in hopes of finding you. I finally find you, married and with a son. You must not have waited long for me to return." Johnny was hurt, and she was questioning *his* love and loyalty?

"The first letter I wrote was within a week or two. I believe it got destroyed when the store with the post office in it burnt down. The next letters I mailed from small towns as I rode express guard for stage companies. They must have taken too long to get there because they were at the post office in Salem when I got back. So, you must have moved out shortly after I left. A real short time in fact." Johnny was showing the hurt and anger that had built up over the years.

"My father insisted that we move and not let anyone know where we moved. He was ashamed to stay and ashamed of me. He thought you were dead. We moved to a farm in Nebraska. We thought the Indian problems were taken care of. Some renegade Cheyenne were on a murder raid. They stopped by our place. Father hid Harry and me in the cellar and he and mother stayed and tried to give them what they wanted. They were angry and drunk. They took what they wanted and killed them both. We were all alone. James came by following after the Cheyenne, him and some other men. Since we were alone, he took us to stay with his family. After a while, I married him because I needed someone to care for Harry and me. He was a good husband to me and good father to Harry. He knew about you and that I still loved you dearly. But we thought you were dead, so we gave Harry his name. We never told Harry any different." Carrie held Trace close to her. "Why do you go by Johnny Rains? Why do you have the reputation of a gunfighter?

"I got into some scrapes and my jobs caused me to use my gun. I didn't want to bring home a name like that to you. My friends in St. Louis know me by both names and why I used them. From St. Louis and throughout the rest of the west, I'm known as Johnny Rains. When I went back to Salem to look for you, I went back as Trace Williams.

"Oh, God, how could this have ever happened to us? Was it punishment for our sin? Carrie just squeezed Trace and cried.

"I guess it was. I was told not to go looking for Donavan and Taggart, but I wouldn't listen. I guess when He said 'vengeance is mine', He really meant it. A town sheriff told me to go home, that even if I found them and killed them, it would change me. Maybe it was better that you found a new life for yourself. I'm sorry about your parents. You said Barton wasn't Harry's father, where is his father?"

Carrie pushed Trace away, with tears in her eyes she asked, "You really have to ask that? Haven't you really looked at him - - his size, his hair, and his eyes; how can you ask that? You really don't know?" Carrie was shocked that he would have asked that. "Why do you think we moved so quickly after you left? Did you forget about the night you left?'

"You mean Harry is my son?" Trace was stunned by

this revelation. He backed into a chair and sat down with his face in his hands. After all the years he missed spending with Carrie and now to find out he had a son raised by another man while he roamed the west by himself. It left him not knowing what to say. Carrie came behind him and pulled him to her and said, "It was a miracle and answer to prayer that you walked into our lives when you did. He needs his father."

For now, just let him know me as Johnny Rains. You have a real problem in Colby. He tried to hire me to help scare you and other ranchers out of the valley. You have more problems coming from him. But, I'm here for you and Harry. I see you named him after your father."

"It was hard for father to accept me having a baby and not married. Mother understood, though I'm sure it hurt her, too. Harry's full name is Harry Thomas Williams. Of course, Thomas is after your father. I insisted on giving him your last name though we weren't married. Then, when I married James, I felt it would be better just to call him Harry Barton. We will have to keep our relationship on a friendship-only basis for a decent amount of time in respect of James."

"Of course, I understand." Trace was standing up to leave.

Carrie put her arms around him and said, "I hope I can remember that. There wasn't a day that I didn't think of you or night I didn't pray that someday and some way the three of us would be together."

Johnny took something from his shirt pocket where he carried Carrie's picture. It was something wrapped carefully in a soft cloth. He unfolded a cloth to reveal a locket on a chain. As he handed it to Carrie, he told her, "This was given to me by a great lady. She's gone now and her husband, also. They became like family to me when I first left to hunt down Donavan and Taggart. I stayed during a snow storm at their home on the way back to you. It was near Christmas and I hadn't anything for you as a gift. Nelly Whitlock was her name; her husband's name was Sam. She gave me this to give to you. When I couldn't find you, I stopped at their place on the way back west. I tried to give it back to her, but she wouldn't take it. She said she would always pray that I would find you. It was special to her; it was given to her by Sam. Their son had died young and they had no one of family to give it to. They thought of me as a son and would have thought of you as a daughter. She would have been happy if you would take it."

"Oh, Trace, it's lovely. It was lovely that she thought so much of you to give it to you. And you kept it all these years. Of course, I'll keep it. I'd never part with it. Oh, Trace, all the years we missed." Carrie broke down and cried. "I am so glad that you had someone like family to you all these years."

"In St. Louis I have a good friend and his sisters who were like a brother and sisters to me. In fact, they still are, and when I got back up to that area I had planned on stopping to see them again."

Harry was tired of waiting to find out what was going on. He walked in to see his mother in the arms of this gunfighter. His anger hit a new high. "Get your hands off of my mother." Still shocked, he said to Carrie, "Mother, it didn't seem to bother you much that he had his arms around you."

"Harry, I told you he is a good friend from a long time ago. He is going to try to help us, so he will be staying here at the ranch. I want you to really get to know him. He would never do anything to hurt us." Carrie was upset. She knew Harry's temperament; he was not a calm person like his father.

Chapter Sixteen

Johnny Takes Charge

The next day one of the hands rode in shouting, "They're running off our stock." Everyone hit the saddles and were on the way to stop the rustling. Coming up on the rustlers, they started shooting. Johnny stopped, stood up in his stirrups and took careful aim. The others kept riding and shooting, missing their shots. They saw one rustler drop off his horse and then a few seconds later another. The other three rustlers quit firing back at the Barton hands and just let the cattle go. Johnny's rifle proved too much for them and also had an effect on the Barton hands. This man knew how to handle the situation. He was something to deal with. He looked at Harry and said "You can be more accurate when you're not bouncing around." Harry had no response.

"Load those two up on their horses; I'll take them back to Colby." Johnny spoke as though he was in charge.

People gathered around the front of the Four Aces Saloon when Johnny Rains rode in leading the two horses with men over the saddles. The sheriff came up to check the bodies; he looked as though he recognized them. "Where did you find them?"

"They were trying to run cattle off the Barton ranch. Their three friends got away. I imagine Colby can tell you the names of the other three. I brought him back these two." Johnny spoke loud and clear, letting it be known that he blamed Colby for the rustling.

"Those are serious charges to make if you don't have any witness that Mr. Colby was there. He's an important man in this town."

"Oh, he wasn't there; he's the type that hires men to do his dirty work. Since you probably work for him, too, I'll leave them here with you."

Colby came to the door of the saloon and stepping out on the porch said, "Strong accusations. Two men are dead and who's to say what they were doing or where they were. Just the word of a gunman. I think that could be questionable. And then you accuse the sheriff of being bought."

"Seven witnesses, Colby. You send out more, and I won't bring them back. I'll leave them for the coyotes to eat. If any of the Barton crew or family gets hurt, I'm coming for you." Looking at the sheriff he added, "And anybody that gets between us."

Turning his horse, he started out of town. Jess Walker said to Colby, "Let me take him now."

"Relax. I have someone coming to deal with him. He should be here in a couple of days." Colby walked back into the saloon.

The next couple of days were uneventful. Johnny tried to get to know Harry better, but didn't get a lot of response from him. Stopping the rustlers made him feel that Johnny was trying to help his mother, but he didn't like the close relationship that seemed to be between them. His father was just gone a few days and here is a man staying at the ranch to help them and wages were not discussed. The ranch couldn't afford the money he could have made with Colby. He heard a lot of stories about this man. Though none were of any illegal dealings or dirty dealings at all, he was deadly to oppose. He had been an express guard, town marshal, sheriff, town tamer, cowpoke and mainly a drifter. He never settled down anywhere that anybody knew. He probably would pull up stakes here in a while and go drifting again. But then, the way he looked at his mother made Harry wonder. The way she looked back and the way they talked for hours - what was the deal? Why hadn't he been around sooner to visit, if he is such a close friend? What would the neighbors and his friends think and say?

After Harry finished fixing the fence, he thought he would take a ride into town. It had been several days since the incident with the Walker brothers. Would they push a showdown with him? He couldn't back down if they did. He wondered if Rains was right, was he out-classed by the Walker brothers. Should he avoid the advice of his friends? Neither of them would try to take on the Walker brothers. Only time would tell and until he finished the fence he couldn't go anywhere.

Harry remarked to Ed that he thought he would ride into town. Ed said he ought to stay out of town; there would only be trouble. Harry's comment was that he couldn't hide forever. Ed told Harry that he couldn't help him against the Walker brothers. They were just too fast for him or Bill. The only one that could help him would be Johnny Rains. Harry remarked that he didn't need his help.

Ed asked why he would say that, adding, "He's a good friend of your mother."

Harry's anger rose at Ed's comment. "Just what did you mean by that? Just because you work for us doesn't give you the right to throw accusations at my mother."

"Now, whoa, boy. Bill and I've been friends of your mother and dad as well as ranch hands. Your mother said that they were friends. He could help you and you'll need it going up against the Walkers. The way you looked at me, you may even need his help going up against me." Ed walked away angrily, his feelings hurt by the comments made by Harry.

Harry realized he was wrong in talking to Ed in the manner he did. He knew that Bill and Ed were really better and more reliable friends than Otis and Freeman, the two he hung out with, would ever be. Hurrying to catch up with Ed, he called out his name and without saying anything he put his hand on Ed's shoulder and walked back to the bunk house with him. Nothing was said, but it was understood.

Ed finally said, "Your mother wants me to go to town tomorrow for some things. Why don't you ride in with me?"

"Sounds good, maybe Johnny will want to ride in with us." Harry made the suggestion without looking up or making an issue of it.

"Maybe he would. You want to ask him or should I?" Ed was trying to make it as easy for Harry as possible.

"When he gets in, I guess I can ask him." Harry left to go up to the house.

The next day the three were riding to town. Ed took the wagon, Harry and Johnny rode their horses. It was a quiet ride, not much talking.

The town seemed quiet and peaceful enough when they arrived. The way people looked at them gave them the feeling something was in the air. Ed said that he would pick up the things at the store and then meet them for a beer before heading back.

As Johnny and Harry walked into the saloon, things got quiet. Looking around the saloon, Johnny saw someone sitting at the table with Colby and the Walker brothers. Seeing the gun belt, he knew that Colby had brought in someone new.

"Mr. Rains, if you have a minute I'd like you to meet my new hand." Colby was showing that he had no idea of changing his way of doing things because Johnny Rains was in town.

It was a surprise when the man turned quickly in the chair and stood up. It was Joe Rollins, Johnny's old friend, now brought in to oppose him in the conflict. The two just looked at each other for a minute. Johnny could see it was a surprise to Joe, also. As they walked towards each other, the people in the saloon backed up out of the way. Each man at the same time put out a hand in welcome of the other. Everyone, including Colby, was taken by surprise at the greeting.

"Johnny, I didn't know you were in town. Colby wired me he needed someone; he didn't say you were here already. Boy, it's been years since we crossed paths. The years have been good to you." Joe showed that the friendship hadn't diminished over the years. "What are you doing here? I hope it doesn't put us on opposite sides."

"If you are working for Colby, it's opposite sides, Joe."

"Is there any way of getting it together; I hate to see us going at one another." Joe showed a real concern about the chance of an outing between him and Johnny.

Harry walked up beside Johnny just as Jess Walker stepped up. "This boy's mama stopped him from drawing on me a few days ago. She isn't here; maybe he'd like to try out Joe Rollins." Jess laughed, trying to edge on Harry to make a challenge to Rollins, which he did.

"If he works for Colby, I'm ready any time he is." Harry's words were out before he had time to consider what he had said.

Joe stepped forward at the remark causing Johnny to step to the side and in front of Harry. "Are you backing the boy? Joe seemed confused as to why Johnny was willing to step in front of this boy.

"I'm asking you to forget what was said and let me handle him."

Johnny turned to talk to Harry, but Harry, realizing they were friends, went back to his thinking that Johnny was with Colby, too. Stepping aside, Harry answered, "What I said I'll back with anyone." Reaching for his gun caused Johnny to move quickly. Johnny's speed showed in the way his hand hit Harry's wrist and with such force that Harry could not draw his forty-five from his holster. Johnny was between Rollins and Harry. Rollins made no move to gun either man. When it looked as if Jess Walker was going to make a play, Rollins turned to face Jess which made Jess stand easy. Rollins had no problem about having his back to Johnny Rains.

"That's kind of dangerous, Mr. Rollins, turning your back on an opponent." Colby was surprised at the reaction of both men.

"I'd trust Johnny Rains with my back any day and any

time. And he's not my opponent; I would never take sides against Johnny. I'm not working for you, if it's against him. I know he has to feel the people are in the right. I never knew a man with more integrity than Johnny Rains; I don't believe I ever will." Joe Rollins threw Colby's money back on the table.

Turning to Harry, Joe said, "Boy, I don't know why he wants to save your life so bad, but be thankful. I'm probably the only one that could come close to taking him. I'm thankful we're friends; I would hate to have to try him. And it's our friendship that stops us; both of us know if it were anything else, it might have happened. Listen and learn from him and you may stay alive and be a man that can walk proud. He is a man of honor."

Harry stood looking at Joe Rollins; he couldn't say a thing. The speed that Johnny showed blocking him from drawing showed that he was no match for him. And he realized, he was probably no match for Joe Rollins.

Rollins looked at Harry and back at Johnny with a questioning look on his face. Then he smiled and said, "Now I know why - the eyes. Johnny, you found Carrie after all these years. I don't think it's a good idea for me to hang around town unless you want me to. So, I gonna be headin' out. Maybe we can meet again sometime and have some dinner and a few drinks." Shaking Johnny's hand and grinning, Joe turned to leave and hit his hand on the back of Harry's shoulder.

Jess Walker hit his hand against Jim's arm and started following Rollins out of the saloon. Jim went out also, but went down along the front of the saloon, as Jess walked out on the street calling to Rollins.

"Rollins, I think you're a coward. I think I can take you, so make your play." Jess was drawing while Rollins back was still to him. Joe figured as much from men like the Walker brothers, so as he jumped to the side as he was pulling his gun. Before Jess could get a good shot at Rollins, he was hit in the chest. The second shot was in the stomach, and it was all that was needed. Jim had pulled his gun to back up Jess, but he never got the chance to use it. A gun barrel was pushing against the side of his head. Johnny had saved Rollins once again from a back shooter. Johnny told Jim to go on out to the street. Rollin said thanks again to Johnny Rains. He told Jim to holster it and make his play any time he was ready. Jim lost all control of himself and started whimpering "I can't draw against you, I can't. You'll kill me."

"You wanted to gun me from the back. I'm giving you the chance to try it like a man. Now make your play, no choice." Rollins held his hands up at his side, giving Jim the advantage. As the crowd stood watching, the sweat poured from Jim's face. Knowing he had little chance, he knew he had to try, but as he said, it was a vain attempt. Both the Walker brothers laid dead in the street.

Colby's top guns were gone; he stood in the doorway looking at Johnny, not knowing what to do. His men are dead; the man he tried to hire is riding out of town. His dreams seemed to be at an end. Johnny Rains stood looking at Colby and then remarked, "Sell what you own around here today. What land you stole from innocent people see that it is deeded back to them. Be out of town in the morning or be waiting in the street.

Colby started stuttering, "You can't, you, you can't."

"Out of town or out in the street in the morning; those are your two choices." Johnny Rains seemed about nine feet tall to Colby and those who heard him, including a young man named Harry. A couple of Colby's men left the saloon and got on their horses and headed out of town. One was the sheriff; he left his badge lying on the bar as he went out. Colby just sank down into a chair, his head in his hands, knowing he had no way out, but to run. Unless! . . .

On the way back to the ranch, Harry had a question for Johnny, "Your friend thought a lot of you. It was plain it wasn't fear in him; I don't think he knows what fear is. What did he mean about my eyes? How did he know my mother's name and how many years you've looked for her?" Harry's mind went back to a time when he was young and setting on his mother's lap. She said he had eyes like his father. He said, "But daddy's eyes are brown." She quickly told him she meant they look at people the same way. It was as though she had been miles away and just got back. Now he is wondering, Johnny has the same color eyes as mine. Mother let him hold her that morning he showed up at the ranch. She seemed to know him by another name. She made them both promise never to fight one another. He realized that he needed a lot of answers.

Back at the ranch, Harry went into the house. Ed and Johnny went on to the bunk house. There was really no conversation being made. Ed looked at Johnny and said, "Do you really think he'll pull out? I can't imagine a man like him giving up everything. I really think he'll buy whatever guns he can to kill you."

"You are probably right, but I have to go in tomorrow and see what he does." Johnny seemed tired. For the first time in a long time he was really concerned with what could happen. He wished right now he and Carrie could just leave and find a place to start over. The desire for him to be up at the house with her right now was strong, but he knew for appearances sake he had to stay a distance from her.

Chapter Seventeen

The Showdowns

Harry had a lot of questions for his mother. When she asked what happened in town and where is Johnny, he told her that Colby had hired a new gun, Joe Rollins. He turned out to be a friend of Johnny Rains. He quit Colby rather than go against Johnny. When Rollins left, Jess Walker called him out. He killed Jess. Jim was going to back shoot Rollins. Johnny stopped him. Then, after Jess went down, Johnny made Jim go out and face Rollins. He didn't want to go up against him face to face, but they made him. He's dead, too. Then Rollins just rode out."

"This Rollins, have you heard of him before?" Carrie was trying to keep the conversation going. It had been hard talking to Harry. He was so tensed up since his father's killing.

"No, but I thought you probably knew him."

"Why would you think that? I don't think I've ever heard the name." Carrie was surprised that Harry would think that she would know someone like that.

"I thought maybe he was just another 'old friend.' He and Johnny are good friends. He knew your name. He looked at my eyes and laughed. Johnny stopped me from trying to draw on him. He probably saved my life, seeing how he took the Walker brothers. I wonder if you know why he said, "the eyes, now I know why you stopped me. You found Carrie." Harry just looked at his mother, then asked, "What did he mean by that, Mother? What haven't you told me? Just who am I?" Harry had laid it on the line. He knew there was more to the Johnny Rains' story than what he had been told.

"Harry, so much has happened lately that I don't know where to begin or how to explain. So many things can happen in life that sometimes we don't know what to do and what is right. Our lives are sometimes controlled by the circumstances we are in. I would never have done anything to hurt you. I think we had better ask Johnny, as you know him, to come up and be with us when we talk. He has much to do with our lives. Please, ask him to come up to the house." Carrie was visibly shaken and upset.

Harry left to get Johnny. As Johnny left, he said to Ed, "I'll talk to you when I get back about what we may be able to do in the morning." Then, he went with Harry to the house. Harry walked with his head down while thinking he half knew what to expect.

Harry held the door and let Johnny walk in. Carrie was sitting in the living room on the couch. She motioned for Harry to sit next to her. Johnny took a chair next to the couch, not knowing for sure what was coming up.

Carrie, with eyes swollen from trying to hold back tears, finally spoke. "Trace, I need you to help me explain to Harry how I know you and the things that have happened in our lives. I don't know if I can handle it by myself."

Johnny, or Trace, as he was going to have to explain, coughed trying to find words to get started. "Your mother and I are from farms that were next to each other near Salem, Indiana. We grew up together. Our parents were best friends, almost like family. I've loved your mother for as long as I can remember. I believed she loved me."

Carrie broke in, "I did, and I do".

"We had planned on getting married. My parents were killed by a couple of drifters. I left to hunt them down. It took longer than I expected. We were very young, about your age. I stayed the night, before I left to find the killers, in your grandfather's barn. Your mother knew how upset I was at losing my parents. We had never really been apart; her family's farm was right up the road from mine. Your mother came out to the barn to spend our last few moments together for who knew how long. The next morning, I left. I wrote your mother, but I believe the letter was destroyed in a fire. The next letters got to Salem too late for your mother and her family to know I was still alive. She found out she was carrying you, and when she told her folks, they decided to move. They were ashamed at her not being married and I had no way of knowing. After finally catching up with the two men, I faced one of them in a saloon; but the other was in back of me. I was in bed in a small town in Colorado for several weeks recovering from the wounds I received in the back. I had left in Mid-April and it was Christmas before I got back. Your mother and her family were gone, no one knew where. She ended up in Nebraska, where her parents were killed. That's where she met James. Your mother was honest with him about you. They married. I just drifted, always looking and hoping to find your mother. I finally found her; she was going into the Four Aces Saloon that night you were going up against Jess Walker. With the problems going on, you losing the man you knew as your father, we thought it best not to say anything until things settled down. Your mother never meant to be untruthful to you; her thoughts were in your best interest. I plan, if I live though the next few days, after a respectful time, to marry your mother if she will have me."

"Harry, I hope you understand. James was a good man; he knew about Trace. We thought he was dead. He was so young to be chasing down the men he was after. I thought it was best for you to go by James' last name. He loved both of us and was proud to let you use his name. My parents were gone, killed by the Indians. I was all alone to take care of you. Please try to understand. I know it's a shock and hard on you." Carrie was worried about the way Harry would take all he was hearing.

Harry was sitting on the couch, his hands together, forearms leaning on his knees. With a heavy sigh, he sat back against the couch and replied, "I really can understand the way you said things happened. I know I wanted to get back at Colby and the Walkers for killing Father. I guess I'm still to call him Father - no disrespect for you, Johnny or Trace or Father, whatever I'm to call you."

"Until we get this mess straightened up, just call me Johnny. Ed and I were talking; we don't believe Colby will take the option of leaving town. He'll probably hire anyone he can to try to ambush me as I come into town to meet him. Ed wants to get some of the other ranchers that Colby is pressuring and come in from the other side of town. The kind of people that Colby can hire now won't like the odds. It will leave him on his own and that he won't like." Johnny knew he had no choice but to meet Colby.

"I guess I'd better get some sleep. It'll be a big day tomorrow. You two probably have a lot to talk over." Saying his goodnights, Harry left the room; he was still a little confused over all he heard tonight.

The morning came quickly to Johnny and the men who were backing him. It was a beautiful morning; the sun warming the morning indicated it would be a hot day. Everyone knew it would be hot in town this morning. As the men rode towards town they were solemn. The men were hoping the show of force would get Colby's men on the run. None of the men looked forward to a gun fight of any kind. They were cattlemen and family men not gunmen, but they had experience fighting either in the war or at times protecting their land and families. Many had fought the Indians, but still, if they could avoid a fight, it would be to their liking.

Colby knew if he didn't win this morning, he was finished. He had hired all the men he could hire to shoot down Johnny before he would have to draw against him. All he had worked for, schemed, connived and killed for, would be lost. He would have to face Rains as though he was going to answer his challenge and hope that his men would cut him down before he could draw his gun. Although it hadn't warmed up that much, Colby was sweating. His life depended on everything working just right. He sat in the Four Aces Saloon waiting, his fingers nervously tapping on the table. Finally, one of the men came in saying that Johnny Rains was riding in.

The streets were empty as Johnny rode in. The main reason for the empty streets, though it was early, was that the town knew that there was be a showdown. Johnny hitched his horse down the street from the saloon. As he started walking down the street, Colby came out of the door of the saloon. Coming down the steps, he called to Johnny, "I decided not to accept your offer. I decided I was here first; you should leave. One way or the other, I believe you said."

"Should have gathered what you had and left; now you leave everything." Johnny let him know that now, there was only one way."

"Look around you." As Colby spoke, he motioned and men stepped out from the alleys and doorways. Colby smiled, knowing he had Johnny hemmed in on all sides. "You think I would let you run me out of town and lose everything. That's your gunfighter mentality. I didn't get to where I am by being run off by words."

"Look behind you. Are you sure your men are ready to die for what you'll be paying them?" Johnny showed Colby a sample of his mentality.

As Colby glanced behind him, he saw Johnny did not come alone like he thought. The men who were backing Colby saw the ranchers and ranch hands with rifles and shotguns ready to do business, if it became necessary. The men on the street in back of Johnny started to get off the streets and some men started backing into the alleys. Colby knew he was finished; the kind of men he hired were not going to go up against so many. Colby was left for a minute without words.

"Mr. Rains, it seems like you have won. I guess I'll have to leave after all." Colby started to go back to the saloon.

"That option was yesterday. You know what the option for today is." Rains had told him to be gone yesterday or face him today. It seemed Colby had played his hand too close.

"What if I don't draw on you? You won't shoot me down in the street. That just isn't you. I'll take my chance on that." Colby knew that Johnny Rains was known as always fair and just; he just wouldn't shoot down an unarmed man or a man that wasn't drawing.

"If you want to walk anywhere, it's to the land office and sign over your landholdings to the people you cheated and ran off. As for your other lands, sign them over to be used for public use until auctioned off. The money will to go to the town for schools, etc. You can leave, alive, with the money in your pocket and your horse and carriage. I think it more than fair under the circumstances."

As Johnny turned to go over to where he had tied up his horse, a shot rang out. Turning with his gun drawn, he saw Colby lying in the street. Ed was standing with his rifle still on Colby, and then looking up at Johnny said, "He was gonna to back shoot you. I'm surprised that you turned your back on him."

"You had my back, didn't you? Why would I worry?" Johnny gave Ed a smile and said, "Let's go back to the ranch"

"Sounds good to me." Ed motioned to the fellows that it was over; they could return to their ranches without the fear of being picked on next to be run out of the area. They all had smiles on their faces and there were many handshakes between them. It was a good day for the town; the man who held so much fear over the town was gone.

As Johnny rode back to the ranch; Harry rode beside him. His mind wandered to the past he had lived and how he wanted to go back to the name of Trace Williams. The people in the town knew him as Johnny Rains. They knew the saying "the storm comes with the Rains." How would he be able to live a peaceful life when there had been so much violence in his past? He always imagined just being Trace when he found Carrie. Now, he also has a son to consider. How many times would some gun show up to get a reputation by being the one who shot down Johnny Rains? He couldn't have Carrie and Harry going through that. Plus, how would Harry be drawn into it? It may be that he would have to move on, after all the years of searching. He didn't want to bring any more harm or hurt to Carrie. He wished he could just bury Johnny Rains.

Chapter Eighteen

The Final Gunfight

Back at the ranch Carrie was waiting on the front porch. She was praying that all her loved ones would come back safely. Besides her son, the man she finally found after all these years, and the men who had worked the ranch with them for years. Ed and Bill were like family. As the riders approached, she stood up to see if all were returning. She thanked God and sighed a sigh of relief that all returned. As Harry and Johnny came up the steps, she took Harry in her arms and took Trace by the hand. She gently started to cry. Harry quietly said, "Everything is ok, Mother, everything is ok."

Everyone took it easy the rest of the day. Only necessary chores were done. Carrie, probably, worked the hardest preparing a meal for everyone and had all the hands eat at the house. Carrie and Trace just talked in generalities, nothing about what was to happen now. Harry just tried to be light-hearted and joked with all the hands. He knew Johnny or Trace, still not sure what to call him, was trying to figure out what would come next. After the meal, Ed suggested that the hands all go to the bunkhouse for a friendly game of poker. Harry added in that he would join them, if Bill wasn't dealing, which had the men laughing and poking fun at Bill.

When they all had left, Trace looked at Carrie and said, "What now?"

Carrie, leaning her head on his shoulder, answered, "We have the rest of our lives before us. I want us to just live in peace, the three of us, until Harry makes it the four of us. You know he's getting to the age."

"Actually, we're still the age to make it the four of us," Trace said with a smile.

"Why, shame on you?" Carrie blushed, still snuggling her head on Trace's shoulder, "What would people think, at our age?"

"Well, probably not much of it, you and a gunfighter."

"But your Trace Williams; you are not Johnny Rains."

"People will always remember me as Johnny Rains, a reputation like that can't be buried."

Carrie, holding tight to Trace as he held her in his arms, said, "I wish there was a way to bury him. Hmmm. Maybe there will be a way for us."

The days passed and life on the ranch went on with everyone accepting Johnny as part of the ranch. Then, one day, a rider came from town with a message for Johnny. A man was waiting for him in the Four Aces Saloon, the same man who had been there earlier to see Colby. The message was for Johnny to wear his guns. Johnny knew there was nothing else to do but answer the challenge that was given. It was part of the life that he was trying to leave. When he told Carrie he had to go to town, she said she needed some things and would go with him. Johnny said no, for her to go later. She knew what it meant. Harry said that he and Ed would ride along with Johnny. Bill could bring his mother in the wagon to get the supplies.

The Four Aces Saloon was crowded. It didn't take long for word to spread when a gunfighter drifted into town. The word had spread that he came to meet Johnny Rains. Joe Rollins was a figure that stood out in a crowd. The way he stood and walked showed that he was no one to reckon with. Some remembered him from his meeting with the Walker brothers. He stood quietly at the bar, just sipping at his drink as though to make it last. Someone quietly said, "Rains is coming into town." Joe Rollins finished his drink and headed for the door.

As he entered the street, Johnny got off his horse and handed the reins to Harry. He slowly walked to the center of the street to face off with Joe Rollins.

"Too many people thought I ran from you the last time I was in your town. I can't live with people thinking that."

"It's better than dying with it." Looking at Rollins, he questioned, "I thought we were friends?"

"We are, Johnny, you never had a better friend, but business is business, so they say. Make your play or I will." Rollins left it clear he was there on business.

There was a silence that hung over the town like a person holding their breath. No one knows who drew first. Both of the men had their guns out so fast that it was hard to tell. It wasn't hard to tell who fired first. It was Rollins' gun that fired fast and even the second shot was fired with no response from Johnny Rains. The first shot must have hit its mark with deadly accuracy. Rains fell and laid on the street without moving. Rollins holstered his gun and started to the saloon. Carrie had just arrived in town with Bill. Harry and Ed went to Johnny's side and as Carrie came over Ed looked at her and said "It's too late; Johnny Rains is dead."

Carrie looked at Joe Rollins as he stood on the steps to the saloon, "I thought you were his friend."

"One of my best. In fact, the only friend I had. I'll miss Johnny Rains."

Bill brought the wagon over and they lifted Johnny Rains into the wagon.

Ed asked Carrie, "Want him buried at the ranch?"

Carrie shook her head, yes, in response.

The town was in shock at the outcome of the fight. Some of the townspeople wanted to be known as friends of the fast gun. They offered to buy Rollins drinks, but he refused. After buying himself a drink, he left to go up to his room.

When Carrie and the three men arrived back at the ranch, Bill drove the wagon into the barn. The ranch hands were gathering around to see what happened. Ed asked a couple of men to dig a grave on the hill alongside James Barton's grave.

It was a private burial, just Ed and Bill doing the burying and Carrie and Harry were there at the time. The men were surprised because they liked Johnny and would have liked to show their respect. But if that's the way Miss Carrie wanted it, it was ok.

After the burial, Carrie and Harry came to the house, and the men continued to do their work around the ranch. A newspaper reporter came out to the ranch. He was going to do a story on "Johnny Raines, Frontier Gun

Fighter." He would appreciate being at the burial and interviewing the last friends of this man who was a legend throughout the west. Ed told him that Raines was already buried and the friends wanted to be left alone. There would be no interviews. The reporter tried to tell Ed that the public deserved the story, but Ed said, "Once and for all, no." The reporter saw that Ed did not want to be bothered any further, so he finally left.

Carrie said she wanted to go into town the next day; she was going to sell the ranch. All the bloodshed was too much and she wanted to take Harry and make a new start. Ed went to town with Carrie and Bill. Now that the trouble was over, it shouldn't be hard to sell the ranch. Ed told the hands that he would see about them staying on at the ranch, or if they wanted to ride for one of the other ranchers in the area, he would put in a word for them. He and Bill were going to go with Harry and Miss Carrie and help them get a new start.

The ranch was sold within a few weeks. Now it was time to get packed up and move on. It was hard giving up the home that James had fought and died to keep, but all things considered, they needed a new home to start over in. After saying good bye to the neighbors and friends, with the wagon loaded and some extra horses to help pull the wagon and to use on the new ranch in Oregon, they started on their journey.

Just outside of town, sitting on his horse as though he was waiting, was Joe Rollins. He tipped his hat to Carrie. She had Bill pull the team to a stop and said, "Mr. Rollins."

Joe politely responded, "Wanted to pay my respects

and say goodbye. I'm going to miss running into my old friend, Johnny. I do wish you and your family the best. It makes me wish that I had a place to call home. I took a job as sheriff in a little town up in Colorado. It may be a start."

"Well, it's about time you change your ways. You looked a little slow on the draw in town a few weeks ago." The voice came from inside the wagon.

Joe laughed and said, "Well, I did the job, didn't I? Remarks like that and I may use real bullets the next time."

Carrie replied, "Yes, you did a good job and I appreciated it, Mr. Rollins. And you, Trace Williams, get your head back in that wagon and don't show your face till we get to Oregon."

Trace laughed and said to Joe, "If you want to change, you can always come to Oregon. There'll be a home for you. Thanks, my friend." Bill started the team again on the way to their new home, all the way to Oregon.

Epilogue

The Bad News and the Good News

In St. Louis, Jake received a telegram. He sent word for his sisters to meet him at the restaurant. He had news for them. When they arrived, he told them he had some bad news for them, but also some good news.

"Girls, Johnny Rains is dead."

Rylee, with tears in her eyes, asked, "What could be good news after that?"

Jake replied, "The good news is Trace found Carrie. They have a son, seventeen years old."

"Well, that is certainly a surprise."

"Sofia!" Rylee was always surprised at Sofia's comments.

"Well, it is."

"What else does it say, Jake?" Rylee knew there must be more.

"They are on their way to Oregon to a new ranch and we're all welcome there whenever we can make it."

"Anything else?"

With a smile on his face, Jake folded the telegram and stuck it in his pocket and said,

"And they lived happily ever after. The End."

LONELY COWBOY
(WITH A DREAM THAT RIDE ALONG)
LYRICS BY CRW

THE CAMP FIRE BURNIN' LOW
AND THE AIR FEELS OF SNOW
IN MY HEART FIRES STILL BURN
AS MY THOUGHTS OF YOU RETURN
STILL YOUR PRESENCE LINGERS ON
THOUGH OUR DAYS TOGETHER'S GONE
I'M JUST A LONELY COWBOY
WITH A DREAM THAT RIDES ALONG
(DREAM THAT RIDES ALONG)

WITH A SADDLE FOR A PILLOW
AND THE HARD GROUND FOR A BED
THE ONLY LIFE A COWBOY HAS
ARE THE DREAMS THAT'S IN HIS HEAD
I HEAR A LONE WOLF HOWLING;
HE'S HOWLING AT THE MOON
WE SHARE THE SAME LONELINESS,
WE SHARE THE SAME OLD MOON
YES, I'M JUST A LONELY COWBOY
WITH A DREAM THAT RIDES ALONG

(DREAM THAT RIDES ALONG)
IN MY SADDLE BY DAY
YOU ARE WITH ME ALL THE WAY
THOUGH THE DAYS ARE LONG AND HARD
IT'S THE WAY I EARN MY PAY
JUST PUSHIN', THE DOGIES ALONG
SAD, LONELY I KEEP A RIDING ON
I'M JUST A LONELY COWBOY
WITH A DREAM THAT RIDES ALONG
(DREAM THAT RIDES ALONG)

I LOOK AT AN OLD TINTYPE
I CARRIED FROM THAT DAY
IT'S BENT AND IT IS FADED
BUT YOUR BEAUTY ALWAYS STAYS
THE PICTURE IN MY MIND OF THE DAY WE SAID
GOODBYE
IS THE PICTURE I WILL CARRY UNTIL THE DAY I DIE
I'M JUST A LONELY COWBOY
WITH A DREAM THAT RIDES ALONG
                    (DREAM THAT RIDES ALONG)

YES, I'M JUST A LONELY COWBOY
(WITH A DREAM THAT RIDES ALONG)

EVERYTHING REMINDS ME OF YOU

LYRICS BY CRW

I HEAR STRUMMING GUITARS
GAZE AT EVENING STARS
AS I HEAR SONGS OF LOVE
THE BIRDS SINGING ABOVE
EVERY SIGHT, EVERY SOUND
IN THE WORLD, ALL AROUND
EVERYTHING REMINDS ME OF YOU

WHEN I THINK OF THE BEAUTY
THE WORLD HAS TO VIEW
THE MORE OF IT I SEE
I KNOW THAT IT'S TRUE
IN ALL THAT I SEE
IN ALL THAT I DO
EVERYTHING REMINDS ME OF YOU

AS I HEAR THE TIDE KISS THE SHORE
I LONG FOR YOU EVEN MORE
THE SOFT GENTLE BREEZE
CARRESS THE LEAVES TENDERLY
THE LOVE IN NATURE ABOUNDS
IN THE WORLD ALL AROUND
EVERYTHING REMINDS ME OF YOU

ON A WINTRY DARK NIGHT
A SUMMER DAY SO BRIGHT
A BLOSSOM-FILLED MAY
COLORED LEAVES BLOWN AWAY
NO MATTER WHAT THE SEASON
YOU ARE ALWAYS THE REASON
EVERYTHING REMINDS ME OF YOU

THE SONGS OF LOVE THAT I HEAR
WORDS THAT SPEAK IT SO CLEAR
HOW CAN MY HEART POSSIBLY HIDE
WHAT I FEEL DEEP INSIDE
IT'S LOVE THAT IS TRUE
IT'S THE MAGIC OF YOU
EVERYTHING REMINDS ME OF YOU

About The Author

I was born in a small house in the little town of Waltersburg, Pa in 1941. Having two older sisters I was lucky to have a good family life. Not the most prosperous, but happy. My first loves of life were westerns, early America stories and music. I spent most of my working years in variety stores. The G.C. Murphy Co. and a few years with McCrory's Stores. Having tried a couple other ventures, I retired from the U. S. Postal Service.

After retiring, I rewrote a short story I had written in the 70's titled "Many Trails". Then I finished a novella that I had started back then titled "the Days of Rains" featured here. I have written many more and I'm presently finishing up another.

I hope that my readers will get the enjoyment out of reading my stories as much as I have reading the stories of others. I thank Kindle and CreateSpace for making possible a means of publishing my books. It is nice to know that people in different countries, such as, Canada, France. Italy, Denmark, England, India and Japan have downloaded copies of my stories. Keep watching for the soon release of my next book.

Thanks to all who have read my stories.

CR Wilson

Made in the USA
Middletown, DE
29 December 2020